Maria
Takes a Stand

© 2004 by Barbour Publishing, Inc.

ISBN 1-59310-357-3

All Scripture quotations are taken from the King James Version of the Bible.

Cover design by Lookout Design Group, Inc.

Published by Barbour Publishing, Inc., P.O. Box 719, Uhrichsville, Ohio 44683, www.barbourbooks.com

Our mission is to publish and distribute inspirational products offering exceptional value and biblical encouragement to the masses.

ecpa Member of the
Evangelical Christian
Publishers Association

Printed in the United States of America.
5 4 3 2 1

A NOTE TO READERS

While the Schmidt family is fictional, other people you will meet in this story really lived. The Uelands were an important family in the history of Minneapolis. Mr. Ueland was an influential attorney, and Mrs. Ueland was active in getting women the right to vote.

During the 1910s, many orphaned children lived on the streets. City newsboys often were homeless and did whatever they could to survive. While the newsboy demonstration in this story is fictional, it represents much of what was happening between company owners and the adults and children who worked for them at that time. The killings in the Ludlow, Colorado, mining camp actually happened. The bad treatment Maria, Curt, and the rest of their family receive as World War I begins is typical of how German-Americans were treated during that time in American history.

SISTERS IN TIME

Maria
Takes a Stand
THE BATTLE FOR WOMEN'S RIGHTS

NORMA JEAN LUTZ

BARBOUR
PUBLISHING

To Will and Rhonda,
with all my love and prayers
for your happiness.

CONTENTS

CHAPTER 1

The Paper Route

Twelve-year-old Maria Schmidt snuggled deeper beneath the heavy quilts layered on top of her. Against her back she felt the radiating warmth of her younger sister Elisabeth, whom everyone in the family called Libby. Maria could tell the temperature outside had plummeted in the night, even though only her nose was out of the covers.

The arrival of March meant spring should be just around the corner, but the storm that hit Minneapolis in the night made it clear that winter wasn't ready to leave just yet. Without opening her eyes, she wondered what had awakened her. She lay there, relishing the sublime feeling of being toasty warm on such a nasty morning.

Blinking once or twice, Maria saw that the electric lamp near the street in front of their house was still lit. Closing her eyes again, she heard soft voices in the narrow hall outside her door, as though Mama was in the boys' room across the hall. Every morning Maria's older brother Thomas and younger brother Curt rose up early to deliver papers on their routes.

Now the knob rattled on the girls' door, and the door scraped against the wooden floor as it opened. Papa kept saying he was going to plane the bottom of the door, but he never found the time. His work at Northwest Consolidated Flour Mill kept him busy from dawn until well after dark each day.

"Maria," Mama's voice whispered.

Maria lifted her head off the soft pillow. "What is it, Mama?"

"Curt has a fever. Will you go help Thomas this morning?"

"I sure will." Sublime comfort was forgotten as Maria crawled over Libby to get out of bed. Since she was older, Maria always slept next to the cold wall just under the eaves. Eight-year-old Libby gave a groan and burrowed deeper into the quilts. Maria pulled on her house shoes and grabbed for her heavy winter wrapper.

"Here." Mama handed Maria an armful of clothing. "Put on Thomas's knickers and wool shirt. Wear your long underwear and put on two pairs of stockings. The snow looks pretty deep."

"Yes, Mama." Maria could hardly believe her good fortune. A pair of Thomas's knickers!

As Mama pulled the door closed behind her, Maria switched on the small globe lamp that sat atop the bureau. The lamp lent a soft golden glow to the small slant-ceilinged room and cast a shimmer on the magazine pages Libby had pinned on the wall. Libby liked to cut out pictures of elegant ladies in pretty dresses and pin them up where she could see them.

Leaning down to peer out the low dormer window, Maria was amazed at just how much snow had fallen in the night. And it was still coming down. She was sorry that ten-year-old Curt was ill, but she was thrilled Mama trusted her to help Thomas with the route. Pulling on Thomas's clothes, Maria thought of all the times she'd told Mama and Papa that she could do anything Thomas did. Now they'd know it was true.

She ran the hairbrush through her pale corn-silk hair, plaited it in one braid down the back, and fastened it up with hairpins. She'd need it to be out of the way. Sitting down on the rag rug, she struggled to pull her shoes on over two pairs of stockings, then fastened the buttons with the buttonhook. In her excitement, she was all thumbs.

By the time she went down the steep narrow stairs, Thomas was at the kitchen door, pulling on his boots. He looked up and gave her his lopsided grin. His blond hair was tousled since he hadn't bothered to comb it yet. "Take the papers out of the toes of my old overboots," he told her. "You'll need them in this mess."

She nodded. The crumpled newspapers in the toes were to make the hand-me-down boots fit Curt. Even without the papers, the overboots were a tight squeeze for Maria. But she didn't care. She wrestled with them until she got them on over her shoes.

Mama stood in the kitchen, cutting up peeled potatoes and placing them in a stoneware bowl. Maria knew there would be fried potatoes and sausage when they got home. Mama was already dressed in her long, black skirt and white shirtwaist, with her hair gathered up into a neat, prim pompadour, ready to go to work. The cameo brooch she wore at her neck had once belonged to Maria's grandmother. Mama was an excellent typist, and because of that, she'd been promoted to head clerk in the offices of the Wynlan Freight Company, which made the family very proud.

"Has Papa gone yet?" Maria asked.

"He just left," Mama said. "And well that he has, too. I shouldn't want to think what he'd say to see his daughter in a pair of knickers."

Maria chuckled. "I think they look great on me!" Thomas handed her Curt's heavy coat and muffler and his hat with the earflaps. As she bundled up, she asked, "How's Curt? Will you call Uncle Robert?" Uncle Robert, Mama's brother, was a doctor. He tended to the various ailments of their entire family.

"A fever and sore throat. I won't bother Robert with that. Nothing that camphor oil can't cure. It's your brother's manly pride that's hurting worse."

Maria knew what that meant. Curt did all he could to keep up with his older brother, whom he adored. And now for Maria to take over his position—she knew it had to hurt.

"Ready?" The muffler wrapped around Thomas's face softened his words. Over his arm were slung the two canvas bags in which they would carry the papers.

"Let's go," Maria answered.

As Thomas pushed the back door open, the wind caught it, and he had to hold tight to push it shut again. Snow was deep even on the back stoop.

"Stay in my tracks," Thomas said. "I'll break the path." At age fourteen, he was almost as big as Papa.

Maria did as he said, keeping her head down against the bitter north wind. It was seven blocks from their house to the *Tribune* building on Washington Street downtown. The tops of the tall buildings disappeared into the low-hanging, snow-laden clouds. By the time they got to the *Tribune* building, Maria was exhausted. Stomping through the snow and pushing against the wind took every ounce of her strength, but she refused to let one complaint slip from her lips.

Thomas led her around to the alley. On the large concrete dock, which had been swept free of snow, men were stacking up rope-tied bundles. Down below in the alley, a pack of newsboys were milling about, slapping themselves on the arms to keep warm as they waited for their papers to be counted out to them. Maria was shocked to see that many of them wore threadbare coats and shoes with holes in the toes.

Of course, Thomas had told her about the street boys who sold papers, and she'd often seen them on their respective street corners hawking the latest news, but she'd never seen them up close. Especially not in such unpleasant conditions. Even with her layered clothing, she was cold. She couldn't imagine how they must feel.

She tried not to stare as two of the boys approached them. They appeared to be Thomas's age or older. One was stocky and barrel-chested. The other was taller and more slender and had a large birth-mark the color of raw liver on the side of his face and extending onto his eyelid.

"Ho, Thomas," the boy said. "You gotcha a new partner there?"

"Where's the kid?" asked the other.

"Curt has a fever," Thomas told them. "This is my sister, Maria. She's gonna help me this morning."

The boy with the birthmark slapped his forehead. "A girl? What? You lost your senses? Ain't no girl can throw papers in this weather."

"Maria can." Thomas's confidence made a warm rush run through Maria in spite of the sharp cold. "Sis," Thomas said, "this here is Anthony."

The stocky boy made a funny bow. "But everyone calls me Tony. I'm leader of these here newsboys." He waved his hand to indicate all the boys in the alley, some even younger than Curt. Tony's chest seemed to puff out as he spoke. "They work the corners that I say they work."

"And I works the best corners right aside Tony." The boy with the birthmark took a step forward.

"This," Thomas said, "is Liver Lid. He can make a news call out of anything and nothing!"

Maria could hardly believe the boy would want to bring attention to the awful birthmark. But he seemed unaffected by the nickname as he stuck out his hand to Maria. His gloves had more holes than fabric. "Pleased to meet'cha."

Maria quickly returned his handshake. "Likewise."

They told her the names of several of the younger boys as well, but she couldn't remember them all. One they called Kicker Joe because when he was younger, he would kick businessmen on the shins while another boy did the pickpocketing.

"A slick team they made, too," Tony remarked. They all laughed like it was a wonderful joke. Maria tried to mask her astonishment.

Just then a man on the dock yelled out, "All right, you little urchins! Time to count out. Listen sharp. I ain't saying nothing twice this morning. It's too cold."

Maria noticed that Liver Lid and Tony moved Thomas right up with them to the front of the line. Thomas motioned for her to stay back. He'd bring her papers to her.

Thomas showed her how to fold the papers and pack them in the bags. The headlines on that day, March 18, 1914, were pretty weak. Maria wondered how the boys would fare trying to sell in the snow with no big news to shout.

Within a short time, Maria's bag was filled with the correct number of papers for Curt's route. The other boys struck out for their street corners, where they would stand and hawk papers until they sold out. Thomas and Maria, on the other hand, went back to their neighborhood, where subscribers had their papers thrown to their front doors.

Other carriers who lived farther away from the news office had their bundles delivered into their neighborhoods. Some of them, Maria knew, had bicycles to ride. While the bikes wouldn't do them much good on a morning like this, Maria still thought it would be great if Curt and Thomas could ride their routes each day. A body could carry more and go farther on a bicycle—and that meant more money.

Quietly, Maria fell into step behind Thomas as he broke the path for her through the powdery snow. Every electric street lamp spread sprinkles of golden light on the snow beneath it. Cold snow sifted down inside her boots as she walked, turning her feet into icicles. When they arrived at the point where the routes began, Thomas turned to her. Pulling down his muffler so she could understand him, he said, "Curt and I usually split up, but he knows every customer. You and I will work together on opposite sides of the street. I'll show you which ones to throw to."

Maria nodded. The weight of the canvas bag cut into her shoulder. All she could think of was lightening the load as quickly as possible.

"We start at the far end and work our way toward home," he explained.

Maria didn't even try to speak. Her mouth was too cold to talk. The biting wind and blowing snow cut like tiny knives. As she trudged along, throwing the papers where Thomas pointed, only the remembrance of his words "Maria can" pushed her on.

Dawn never really came that morning. The skies simply grew a lighter shade of dense gray. Maria suddenly realized it was no longer dark, just as she realized her bag was no longer full. She'd done it! She'd actually thrown an entire newspaper route. And in a snowstorm to boot! As they turned toward the house, she felt light and giddy inside. Instead of following in Thomas's path, she pushed out ahead of him in a burst of energy and started kicking snow into the air.

"Hey, watch it!" he called through his muffler.

"I'll beat you to the house," she called back once she had a good head start.

"You're on!"

She squealed as he gained on her. She was running through the path they'd made earlier, but he circled out around her, passed her, and still beat her home. As they reached the back steps, she could hardly catch her breath from laughing so hard.

Opening the back door for her, Thomas said, "Thanks for helping, Maria. You're a trooper."

"You're welcome. Say," she said, punching him in the shoulder, "if Mama's already left for work, maybe I could wear your knickers to school!"

"Over my dead body."

CHAPTER 2
Aunt Josephine,
the Suffragette

The kitchen was all steamy and warm, bursting with the aromas of hot coffee and fried sausage and potatoes. Mama hadn't left yet. Libby was up and dressed in her winter school dress. She lifted the black graniteware coffeepot and filled the mugs, then dished up breakfast for her older siblings. Meanwhile, Mama was tying on her heavy knitted hat, which looked rather like a ruffled bonnet.

"I hope the trolley's on time in this deep snow," Mama worried as she pulled on her leather gloves. Papa walked to the flour mill every day, but he insisted they invest in the trolley for Mama.

"Mayhap my wife must go to work," he'd say, "but walk to work she will not."

"I saw them clearing the tracks over on Nicolett Street," Thomas said as he shook snow off his coat and hung it up on the hooks by the back door. "You might cross over a street and wait there."

"I'll do that, Thomas. Thank you."

"Your breakfast's on," Libby said.

"Thanks, Libby." Maria stepped to the sink to run water over her hands to bring feeling back to her fingers. "Mama, may I wear Thomas's knickers to school? The snow's terribly deep."

A gasp escaped Libby's lips. "Maria! Thomas's knickers?"

Mama didn't react so violently. She simply said, "Of course not,

Maria. What a silly question. Eat your breakfast and get changed quickly so you won't be late for school. Your knitted petticoat will keep you warmer even than knickers." She kissed each one of them and stepped toward the door. "Be sure to speak to Curt before you leave."

Thomas stepped to the door to help her against the wind. Mama turned and said, "We all appreciate you taking Curt's place, Maria."

"Pleased to help," she answered politely. What she wanted to say was, "If I can throw his papers, why can't I wear knickers to school?" But she bit her tongue and swallowed the words.

She turned to the mirror above the sink where Papa shaved each morning. His leather strop hung on a nail close by. The mirror was an old one, small and sort of greenish with brown spots where the silver had worn off on the back. She glanced at her plain face and her too-big nose. *A face much better suited to be a boy's than a girl's,* she thought.

After breakfast, Maria changed into her school dress and slipped into Curt's room to tell him good-bye. On the wall of the boys' bedroom hung two flyers. One was a travel advertisement that said, "See the Wild West." The second was an advertisement for a real Wild West show that had come through town a year ago. Horses were a source of constant fascination for Curt. He would even pet the old nags in town that were hitched up to delivery drays. Curt was quiet, but when he did talk, he talked about cowboys and horses.

Maria looked at his face as he lay beneath the covers, his cheeks pink from fever. His dark tousled hair was the color of Papa's. He was probably dreaming about riding across the wide-open range that very moment. She knelt down by his bedside.

"We're about ready to leave, Curt," she said softly. "Anything you need?"

His dark lashes fluttered then, and his wide blue eyes looked at her. "I thought you were already gone."

"We wouldn't leave without telling you good-bye."

"I heard you leave earlier."

"I helped Thomas throw your paper route."

"You did?"

She nodded. "It's very hard work, Curt. I don't see how you do it. I'm so proud of you."

He smiled. "Did you meet the boys? Tony and Liver Lid and all of them?"

"I did."

"They like me. I'm their friend and so is Thomas. Tony had a pet mouse one time, and he let me hold it."

Maria gave a little shiver at the thought. "I'm glad you're friends with them." She leaned over and kissed his hot forehead. "I'm going now, but I'll come home during lunchtime to check on you." She tapped the glass of water on the small spindle-leg table by the bed. "I'm leaving your water right here."

"Thanks, Maria. Tell Thomas good-bye for me."

"Tell him yourself," she said, pointing to the door.

"What about me?" Thomas entered with Libby on his heels. Both were dressed in their heavy coats and mufflers.

"Sorry I couldn't help this morning, Thomas," Curt told his older brother. "Real sorry. I woulda come, but Mama said not."

"Mama was right," Libby said in a motherly tone. "It's right nasty out there."

Maria slipped out of the room and downstairs to get her coat and muffler on. As she pulled on her knitted hat, she figured that if Curt grew worse, she'd stay home with him that afternoon. Mama might not be able to take time off work, but it wouldn't hurt if Maria missed a little school time.

Thomas walked only halfway with the girls before turning off to Central High School, where he attended. Libby and Maria then had to make their own path to Washington Elementary. If Curt had been with them, he'd have thought it was his duty to break the path. Maria did it instead, walking ahead of Libby and doing a fair job of it, even though she was getting most of the snow down her overboots. How she wished she were still dressed in knickers. Boys were so lucky.

Several eighth-grade boys were shoveling the school sidewalks when they arrived. Every once in a while, one boy would dump a shovelful of snow on another, which resulted in a wild wrestling match.

"Boys!" Libby said in a disgusted tone.

Maria thought the rowdiness looked to be great fun. She usually stayed out on the playground until the bell was rung, but she'd about had her fill of snow and cold today.

Inside the seventh-grade room, the steam radiators hissed as they pumped at full pressure. Some of the girls had placed their wet woolen mufflers on the radiators to dry, and the room smelled like damp wool.

Cathy Wyatt and Evelyn Moore and that bunch were standing close by the radiator in the farthest corner of the room, talking and giggling. They paid little attention to Maria, and she returned the favor. Just because their fathers were successful businessmen and just because they had a few nicer things to wear, they seemed to think they were something special.

Maria went into the cloakroom to hang up her things. The wooden floor was wet with puddles from snow melting off all the overboots. Mr. Jameson had scheduled a geography test for that day, and last evening Thomas had helped her study. She was sure to make an A.

As Maria came out of the cloakroom, Charles Briggs made a face at her. "Has your aunt Josephine been put in jail yet?" he asked. "Are you going to be the niece of a jailbird?"

Maria walked past him as though he'd not said a word. The silly statement didn't deserve one bit of her attention. Several kids snickered, and another boy picked up the taunt, "Jailbird. Jailbird. All them suffrage dames should be tossed in the clink."

Cathy and her friends in the back of the room snickered as though on cue. Only Torvald Ueland didn't join in the laughter. The quiet Norwegian boy who sat in Maria's row always behaved himself no matter what mischief happened in the room. Although Maria didn't know him well, she respected him.

Taking her seat, she opened her geography book to review her notes. Charles would probably flunk the geography test as he usually did. Why should a dummy like Charles be able to vote one day and Maria not have that same right? She was a whole lot smarter than Charles Briggs.

It had only been a few months since Aunt Josephine joined the suffrage association in Minneapolis. Maria was proud of her aunt for joining and proud of Uncle Robert for allowing her to do so. How Charles Briggs found out about Aunt Josephine was anyone's guess, but such gossip did spread quickly. Obviously, he'd heard about the suffragettes in Washington, D.C., who were being arrested and thrown in jail.

Just then, Mr. Jameson came breezing in the door, smiling as usual. "This is not a good day to be the owner of an automobile," he said with a laugh. "Even after I dug her out of the snow, my old tin lizzie just stood there and refused to turn over."

Charles, suddenly the picture of perfect behavior, rushed up to take Mr. Jameson's book satchel. "Here, sir. Let me help."

"Thank you, Charles." Mr. Jameson pulled off his hat and muffler and hung them just inside the cloakroom on the special peg that was his. "And anyway," he continued, pulling a comb from his pocket and slicking down his curls, "as I came in on the trolley, I saw the folks who did get their autos started. They were stuck in drifts all along the way. Give me a horse and sleigh in winter every time."

The students laughed because Mr. Jameson didn't even own a horse, let alone a sleigh. Soon their teacher was assigning the morning Scripture reading, which was followed by prayer, the flag salute, and singing the national anthem. Evelyn and Cathy took turns playing the upright piano for the morning singing. Both took lessons, of course. Evelyn was a fair pianist, but Cathy still made plenty of mistakes. Maria smiled to herself whenever it happened, but only because Cathy acted like she was better than anyone else in the class, and Maria knew for sure she wasn't.

When it was time for the geography test, Maria saw the scowl on Charles's face. After Mr. Jameson asked that books be put away and the tests were handed out, she saw Charles craning to look over Anna Davis's shoulder. Anna, bless her soul, was hunched over her paper. She'd probably noticed him looking on her work before.

Maria flew through the test, remembering all the clever ways Thomas helped her to remember names and dates. Thomas said she had a quick mind. *A quick mind,* she thought as she took her paper to Mr. Jameson's desk to hand it in. A great compliment from her smart older brother.

As she returned to her seat, Maria took her library book from her desk and enjoyed the story while the others finished. But her mind was still on Aunt Josephine. How Maria wished she could serve in the suffrage association as well. It would be a crying shame to leave the future of the country in the hands of someone like Charles Briggs.

CHAPTER 3
At the Andersons'

When Maria went home at lunch, Curt's fever seemed worse. She decided to stay home with him. First, though, she ran next door to Mrs. Braun's to borrow the telephone, wiping the snow from her boots carefully at the back stoop.

Mrs. Braun's house was scrubbed clean as a shiny nickel. Mama said Mrs. Braun followed her husband, Johann, from room to room wiping up his foot tracks. Mama said it in jest, but Maria wondered if it weren't more truth than fiction.

Maria called the school to say she was staying home with Curt, then called the high school office to leave a message for Thomas to fetch Libby so their sister wouldn't walk home alone.

"Danke schön, Mrs. Braun," Maria said as she left. "I'll ask Thomas to shovel your sidewalk as soon as he comes home from school."

"Ya, Maria. I vould like dat very much. By the time Johann shuts up der leather goods shop, iss too dark to see der shovel."

Maria nodded. "I know. It's very dark when Papa comes home, too."

The blustery weather made home seem cozier than ever to Maria. Through the afternoon, the hand-carved German clock that hung in the parlor kept her company. The little man and woman came out and danced as a lilting polka melody played, then the clock bonged the hours. The beautiful clock was one of the only things Papa had received when his parents had died. All the other things that had come from the Old Country went to his older brothers.

Maria made a pot of soup for supper. When she took a bowl of the soup upstairs to Curt, he was deeply immersed in a book. Next to horses, Curt was partial to books—even when he was sick. Mama said Curt would rather read than eat, and it was true. This dime novel was called *The Call of the Canyon,* which sounded quite boring to Maria.

After he'd eaten the soup, she asked, "Want to come downstairs? I can fix a bed on the divan."

"May I bring my book?"

Maria smiled. "Can't imagine you without it."

She'd no sooner said it than he grabbed another book from beneath his pillow, *The Boss of the Lazy Y.*

"Let's go," he said.

Maria was sure Curt was feeling better.

At supper he was able to sit at the table with the family even though his cheeks were still flushed.

"Did I do right to stay home with Curt?" Maria asked Mama. Now that the sparkle had returned to her little brother's eyes, she wondered if he'd stayed home just to avoid school.

Mama and Papa exchanged glances as they often did before one of them answered the children. Papa had washed the white powdery flour from his face and hands, but short of a full bath, he never could quite get it all out of his dark hair and mustache. With a smile he said, "To have a tasty pot of soup already cooked for supper on such a blustery day, Maria, a blessing it would be to have you home every day."

"Now, Franz," Mama chided him, "don't tempt her." Mama then said, "Why don't we ask Curt his opinion?"

After tipping his bowl to get the last spoonful of soup, Curt said, "I started perking right up when Maria said she was staying with me. Being sick is worser when you're all alone."

"There you have it," Mama said.

"Aw now, Curt, I bet your nose was so deep in a book you didn't know if you were alone or not," Thomas teased.

Curt grinned and tossed his head to shake the long hair out of his eyes. "I was reading, but I was still lonely 'til Maria came. She let me come down to the divan."

"Wish I coulda been here, too," Libby said, not wanting to be left out.

"What?" Thomas said in mock surprise. "And miss the piggyback ride through the snow?"

Maria looked at her brother. "You carried her piggyback? Wasn't that quite a load?" After all, Libby was quite a bit heavier than their young cousins Lloyd and Joanne, who often received piggyback rides from both Maria and Thomas.

"I carried her only a short way," he said. "It was fun. Or at least *I* thought it was."

"I'm sorry, Thomas," Libby said, her eyes lighting up at his teasing. "Riding on your back truly was fun."

"Will I go to school tomorrow?" Curt asked.

Mama looked at Papa again. "What do you think?"

"A safe bet would be one more day inside," Papa said.

Curt groaned. "But my route."

"I can do it again, Curt." Maria tried not to let the excitement bubble up through her voice. "I'm not taking your work away from you. I'm only your substitute."

Curt seemed satisfied with this.

"Speaking of substitutes," Papa said, "the secretary of our workers' union is quitting his position. The men want me to put my name in as a candidate."

Mama was quiet, but Maria saw her purse her lips tight.

"Will you do it?" Thomas asked.

"I'm considering it."

Quiet followed. Each of them knew how the management of the mill hated the unions. According to them, union members were nothing but troublemakers. Papa had been a member for a time, but never an officer.

Mama spoke with more calm than she was probably feeling. "When we say our prayers this evening, this matter will definitely be included."

At the newspaper office the next morning, Maria was again greeted by Tony and Liver Lid and the other boys. Liver Lid jabbed Tony playfully in the ribs. "If them headlines today is something that'll sell fast," he said, "then we'll shovel a few sidewalks for an extra nickel or two."

"That we will," Tony answered. "Enough to buy supper tonight. Sure can't shine any shoes in this mess."

The sight of the younger boys dressed in ragged clothing filled Maria with sadness. While the Schmidts didn't have much money, they at least had warm clothes and a mama and papa to remind them that God loved them. These boys had so little.

Dozens of wealthy men dressed in heavy wool coats and fancy bowlers probably passed the boys every day and never saw their need. What was it about wealth, Maria wondered, that blinded people to the poor around them? If she had money, there'd be breakfast for them every morning. And warm mittens for all the stiff, red, cold fingers. And she'd never let them forget that God loved them.

Throwing Curt's route that morning was easier since many of the walks had been shoveled. And although it was bitter cold, at least there was no snow biting her face. As Thomas pointed where she should throw, Maria formed a plan. If she helped her brothers every day, they could increase the routes by half again as much. What fun it'd be to wear a pair of Thomas's knickers every day and work alongside the boys. She'd ask Mama the first chance she got.

But Mama wouldn't hear of it. "It's boy's work," she said. "The *Tribune* would never give a route to a girl, so it's out of the question."

Maria had found Mama alone in the kitchen just before they were to go visit Uncle Robert and Aunt Josephine that Friday evening. Maria hadn't thought Mama would be so vehement about the matter.

"They wouldn't need to give me a route," Maria protested. "If the boys asked for more territory, then I could help throw."

Mama was shaking her head before Maria got the last word out. "The answer is no. And I know it would be the same from your papa. The matter is closed."

Maria didn't want to argue with Mama, but she couldn't understand why she was able to throw Curt's route when he was sick, but not every day. Why were people always thinking of rules about what girls could and couldn't do? Same way with the vote. Maria believed everyone should be allowed to vote. Men and women alike.

Aunt Josephine's parlor never showed a speck of dust in spite of having three little ones dashing about. Maria breathed deeply of the sweet aromas of beeswax and turpentine, which had been used to make the oak floors glow. They'd all gathered in the parlor after dinner. For once they finished dinner without Uncle Robert being called away. His black bag was always on the front hall table, ready at a moment's notice.

Aunt Josephine had given Libby a past issue of *Ladies Home Journal*, and she was sitting at a small table, scissors in hand, cutting out pictures of ladies dressed in the latest fashions. Besides pinning the pictures on her bedroom wall, Libby created paper dolls from them and played for hours. On the floor nearby, Curt and six-year-old Lloyd played with Lloyd's collection of wind-up toy automobiles.

"So," Uncle Robert was saying to Papa, "have you decided then? Will you be a candidate for secretary of your labor union?" Uncle Robert had a soft, gentle, doctor-kind of voice. He was used to talking kindly to sick folk.

"Someone must do it, Robert. If not, there never will come the day when workers have a say in matters."

Uncle Robert shifted position in his overstuffed chair, being careful not to disturb the sleeping four-year-old Joanne in his lap. Her dark hair, much the same color as her father's, curled about her pretty face, making her look like a little china doll.

"Do you think it wise, Franz," Uncle Robert remarked, "to make yourself so visible? They know how to target people. Is it worth the risk?"

"To stand for what is right? It is worth it," Papa replied.

Papa's German accent was more noticeable when they were with the Andersons than when they were with all Papa's relatives at a big German *saengerfest* or one of the many German festivals they attended. Sometimes Maria felt like two different people—one very German, the other not-so-German. One day she asked Thomas if he ever felt that way, but he said he'd never thought about it. He was American, and that was that.

As the wife of a German man, Mama did well to cook most of the foods that Papa liked, but she never really liked going to the noisy *biergartens* on Sunday afternoons. To Mama, Sunday was for being quiet, not for drinking beer and listening to the oompah-pah of a rousing German polka band.

But Papa didn't drink beer. He said he went because it was his time to be with home folk and to learn news of the Fatherland, as he still called Germany. For that reason, many Sunday afternoons found the Schmidt family with the rest of the German population of Minneapolis, many of whom were their relatives. Those were the times when Maria felt most keenly that she wasn't really German at all.

She was proud of the resoluteness she'd heard in Papa's voice when he spoke of the labor union. But then she happened to glance over at her younger brother. Curt the worrier, she sometimes called him. She could see concern in his young eyes. Thomas, on the other hand, looked as pleased as Maria felt.

"I agree with Franz," Aunt Josephine was saying. "We do need to stand up for what's right. That's what compelled me to join the suffrage group."

Maria had snuggled comfortably into a corner of the pillow-laden divan. She didn't usually enter into the adult conversation, since all the children had been taught to be seen and not heard. But her words spilled out almost before she could think.

"A boy at school asked me if you were going to jail, Aunt Josephine. Will you go to jail for helping women get the vote?"

Aunt Josephine had a light, happy laugh, and it filled the room. "Oh, dear me, no, Maria. I'll not be going to jail. At least I don't plan on it. I'm not too sure I agree with all the shenanigans of Miss Alice Paul and her group at the capital. They're the ones who've been taken to jail. We're a bit more conservative here in Minneapolis."

Turning to Mama, Aunt Josephine said, "That reminds me, Christine. Mrs. Ueland happened to say at our last meeting that we need more women from the workplace added to our numbers."

"Mrs. Ueland?" Mama said. "Who's she?"

As Aunt Josephine moved, the lamplight accented the red highlights of her strawberry blond hair. "Clara Ueland," she said. "Wife of Andreas Ueland, the attorney."

Mama nodded, but Maria was sure her mother had never heard of the Uelands. "Their son Torvald is in my class," Maria offered.

Mama nodded again.

"Clara is head of the Equal Suffrage Association of Minneapolis," Aunt Josephine continued. "She's a dear friend. You would like her."

Maria wasn't sure about that. She couldn't imagine Mama being friends with such wealthy, prominent citizens as the Uelands.

"At any rate, Clara feels it's time to draw on our working sisters in the city. That's where you come in, Christine. Would you help us form a suffrage group at Wynlan's? I can't think of a better place to begin in all the city."

Mama never answered quickly to anything. She sat quietly thinking while Maria was about to burst. What a privilege it would be to gather support for the suffrage movement. At last Mama asked, "What would it entail?"

"You'd begin by handing out literature and procuring names and addresses of those who are supportive of our cause. Then you'd encourage them to attend our monthly meetings. Often our speakers are women like Carrie Chapman Catt. They give rousing talks and spur us on to work even harder for the vote."

Maria had never heard of anything so exciting. If she were Mama, she'd say yes in a heartbeat. But all Mama said was, "I'll think about it, Josephine. I'll think about it."

CHAPTER 4

Learning to Be a Lady

Sounds of hammering rang out from the Schmidts' backyard. Maria sat on the back stoop with her arms wrapped around her knees, watching as Thomas made Curt a pair of wooden stilts.

The April sunshine promised much but delivered little. The air was still too cool to be without a jacket. The first green sprigs of grass were poking through, although not much grass grew in the packed dirt of their small backyard. Mama was able to make a few marigolds and petunias come up along the fence each year, but that was about all.

Absently, Maria scratched her legs and wondered how soon Mama would let them stop wearing their long underwear. A few more sunny days like this, and she might say yes.

For the past week, Thomas had tromped all over the neighborhood on his pair of stilts, with Curt following close behind begging to try. Thomas finally let him, and once Curt got the hang of it, there was nothing to do but make a pair for him as well.

Curt held a small block of wood, where a person's foot was to be placed, while Thomas drove in the nails. That morning the boys had made a trip to the dump to find more boards. Maria had begged Mama to let her go, but Mama needed her to do the Saturday cleaning while Mama went to work. Libby and Maria willingly helped with the cleaning, of course, but it still didn't seem fair. Boys had all the fun!

"Why would you want to go to a smelly old dump?" Libby had asked Maria.

Neat-as-a-pin Libby would never understand. Just going to the dump wasn't what mattered to Maria. Actually it *was* a smelly place. But boys always got to do adventurous things, while she was stuck with dull things like cleaning house and cooking dinner. Now the house was spotless, and Papa's favorite bread was baked and ready for supper. So Maria allowed herself a few minutes to come out and soak up the sunshine.

"Hold it steady," Thomas said as he raised the hammer again.

"I'm holding it as steady as I can," Curt replied.

"Need some help?" Maria stood and sauntered closer to watch. "I can help hold."

"Naw," Curt said, "I've got it." But the board did slip when Thomas's hammer came down hard.

"Let's let her hold that end." Thomas looked up at Maria and gave her his lopsided smile.

"Well, all right. Just the end," Curt agreed.

The wood was splintery, but Maria used the hem of her skirt to protect her fingers. Once she got a good grasp, she held on hard. With her help, the stilts were finished in no time.

"Take them to the stoop," Thomas directed. "It'll be easier to get up on them."

"I know, I know," Curt said. "I've walked on yours, don't forget." At the stoop, Curt steadied first one stilt and then the other and quickly was up and going. "Whee, I'm taller than all of you," he called out as he walked around the yard, lifting first one and then the other of the wooden stilts.

"May I try yours, Thomas?" Maria asked.

"Think you should?" he replied.

Libby came out on the porch carrying her china-faced doll with the painted-on black hair, a Christmas gift from Aunt Josephine that was Libby's favorite possession. She had named the doll Florence after Florence Lawrence, an actress in the moving pictures. Mama said she should have named her doll after a Bible character such as Ruth, but Libby was adamant, and the name stuck.

Libby had caught the drift of the backyard conversation. "Maria, you're not supposed to walk on stilts," she protested. "That's for boys."

"Yeah," echoed Curt, coming back nearer the house and still keeping his balance perfectly. "For boys."

"I can do whatever a boy can do," Maria countered. She wanted to remind Curt of how she threw all his newspapers in a driving snowstorm, but she knew that would hurt his feelings.

Thomas was saying, "Tuck up your skirt, sis. Let's see how you do."

Good old Thomas. She could have hugged him. As he brought his stilts over to the stoop, she tucked up her dress hem, making the skirt like a pair of bloomers. She stood poised at the edge of the stoop, and Thomas helped her step up on the wooden supports.

"I'll steady you 'til you get the hang of it," Thomas offered. "That's what I did with Curt."

Walking on stilts wasn't as easy as it looked. Maria wobbled some. But then she got the feel and rhythm—lift one and set it down, lift the other and set it down. Thomas stepped back and let her go.

"I'm doing it!" she called out. "Do you see me, Curt? Libby? I'm really doing it."

"You're doing fine," Thomas called out. "Just watch out for. . ."

In a split second, one of the stilts sank down into soft dirt, throwing her off balance. As she crashed to the ground, she heard a ripping sound, but she was more aware of being unable to breathe. The wind had been knocked clear out of her.

"The gopher holes," Thomas said, finishing his sentence.

"What'd I tell you?" Curt jumped nimbly down from his stilts and ran over to see if he could help.

Thomas was already beside Maria, helping her to sit up. "Are you all right?"

"Mama's gonna be real mad you tore your dress." Libby stood, looking down at her older sister with a measure of disdain.

When she could breathe again, Maria looked at Thomas. "I did it, didn't I?" she managed to say between gasps.

"I have to admit it. You did."

"If it hadn't been for the gopher hole. . ."

"You'd still be up there," Thomas said.

"Well," she said struggling to her feet, "since I know where the gopher hole is, let me try again."

"Don't you think that's enough for one day?" Thomas touched her arm where it was scratched and bleeding. It must have hit the wood on her way down.

"Mama's gonna be mad about the dress," Libby repeated.

"I can sew up the dress," Maria reminded her, tucking the hem up once again. She took the stilts to the stoop, got up without any help, and made her way around to the front sidewalk. Maria walked a ways up and down the sidewalk. No gopher holes there. The exhilaration of standing higher than anyone else was surpassed only by the exhilaration of doing something that only boys were supposed to do!

Just then, Mrs. Braun opened one of her front bay windows, stuck her head out, and yelled, "Maria Schmidt! Ach! My eyes cannot believe what they are seeing. A fine young lady like you! You should come down off those crazy sticks this instant."

Startled, Maria wobbled a bit, but she quickly caught her balance and kept on walking. What business was it of Mrs. Braun if she walked on stilts or on the ground? How could it make any difference to anyone?

Thomas, Curt, and Libby would never have told on Maria, but that evening Maria caught sight of Mrs. Braun accosting Mama as she came home from work. From Mama's expression, Maria guessed that her mother was not terribly pleased with the news.

When Mama finally got home, she took off her wraps and pulled the long hat pin from her felt hat. She hung the hat on the hook by the back door along with her coat. "Come into the parlor, Maria," she said. "Let's talk."

For once, Maria was glad Papa came home late. At least she would only have to face Mama.

Mama sat in Papa's Morris chair and motioned for Maria to sit on the nearby divan. "Now what's all this about you making a spectacle of yourself in front of our house?"

"I walked on Thomas's stilts. And I did well at it, too," she said.

Mama was quiet. She picked up Papa's reading glasses from the table beside his chair, the pair he wore when reading the Bible, the newspapers, and all his German publications. Putting the glasses on, Mama picked up the Bible and placed it in her lap.

The carved clock chose that moment to begin its happy little serenade, and the couple did their skittery little dance. The gong sounded six times.

"Doing wrong is one matter," Mama said when it was quiet again. "Being proud of doing wrong is yet another."

Maria didn't feel she'd done anything wrong, but she couldn't say that. Not to Mama. So she kept quiet and waited.

"Is that how you tore your dress?"

Maria had neatly stitched it, but it was a long rip. Right in front, near the hem. Mama's eagle eyes missed nothing. Maria nodded.

"When you asked to go to the dump with the boys this morning, what did I tell you?"

Maria tried to remember. "You told me I couldn't go with them."

"What else did I say?"

"You said the dump was no place for a lady."

"Precisely. And being precariously perched on a pair of stilts in front of all the neighbors is no place for a lady, either."

"But, Mama," Maria blurted out, "it's so unfair that boys get to do things that girls can't do. Just because I'm a girl, I'll never even get to vote, and I'm a whole lot smarter than that silly old Charles Briggs. I wish I'd been born a boy!" She hadn't meant to be disrespectful, but the words kept tumbling out.

"I don't believe this conversation is about voting or about Charles Briggs. We're talking about your discontent." Mama opened the Bible to the book of Romans. "You are not the potter, Maria Schmidt. You are the clay." Adjusting the glasses, she said, "Romans 9:20 says, 'Nay but, O man, who art thou that repliest against God? Shall the thing formed say to him that formed it, Why hast thou made me thus?' "

Carefully, Mama unhooked the reading glasses from behind her ears and placed them back in the black leather case. The case snapped shut. "God created you to be a lady, and God doesn't make errors. Even without speaking, your actions question God's wisdom in this matter."

Maria stared at Mama's Franklin treadle sewing machine pushed up against the wall. The machine was covered with one of Mama's dainty tatted coverlets. Maria couldn't deny that she'd questioned God. Surely He *must* have made a mistake. Deep inside, she was still certain she was as good as any boy alive.

"Before you return to school on Monday," Mama continued, "you will write this verse one hundred times and turn in the pages to me."

"Yes, ma'am."

But even as she spent hours that evening at the kitchen table writing, Maria decided that if God hadn't made a mistake, perhaps it was the people around her who were wrong. In what she'd read of the Bible, she found nothing about girls not walking on stilts—or not going to the dump, for that matter. Who made all the silly rules anyway? Perhaps when she got a little older, she could help change a few.

Thomas sat at the table with her doing his schoolwork. He'd

already apologized for helping her to get in trouble.

"Please don't apologize, Thomas," she said. "Because of you I know now that I truly can walk on stilts. But I probably should have stayed in the backyard."

Thomas gave his lopsided smile. "Don't forget, Mrs. Braun can see our backyard as well."

Curt came home from his delivery run one morning upset about the news. He'd even used his own money to purchase a copy of the paper. The article told of miners near Ludlow, Colorado, who had gone on strike because they wanted better safety conditions in the mines. One accidental explosion had killed seventy-six miners.

The article explained that when the miners went on strike, the company evicted the strikers and their families from their company houses. The miners had created a tent city for temporary shelter through the winter months. They and their families had suffered from cold and hunger. Finally that spring, the infantry and cavalry had been called in. Instead of helping the cold and hungry families, the soldiers were under orders to force the miners to return to work.

Curt read the story aloud as Mama prepared to leave to catch the trolley. It told how four men and a boy were shot dead. Then the tents were set on fire. Twelve children and two women who were hiding in a space under one of the tents died from smoke inhalation. The miners were forced to return to work. Nothing had been gained.

"Sometimes I wonder if reading all the news is healthy," Mama said as she pulled on her coat and pinned on her hat.

"You're supposed to be throwing those newspapers," Maria said to Curt, "not reading them."

"I can't help but see the headlines," he protested. "Why would the army kill innocent people just because they were striking for safer working conditions? Why? It doesn't make any sense."

"There are many things in this world that don't make sense," Thomas said. "Shouldn't you be eating your breakfast?"

Curt sat down at his place, but he just picked at the sausage and eggs.

Mama kissed each of her children good-bye but lingered at Curt's place, giving him a special hug. "Those brave people were doing what they thought to be right, Curt. Who knows? Perhaps their sacrifices will cause changes to come about." She pointed to the article. "If their plight is published in papers across the nation, perhaps public opinion will shift in favor of the workingman. There may come a day when the millionaire business owners can no longer mistreat their workers, nor sway government officials to their side."

After Mama had gone out the door, Maria thought about what she'd said. She'd never heard Mama say that about making sacrifices before. Perhaps that meant Mama would help Aunt Josephine in the work of the suffrage association. Mama's sacrifice might also help changes to come about.

On the way to school, Libby pointed out to Maria all the pretty dresses the other girls were wearing, especially the girls whose fathers dropped them off in their fancy touring cars. Now that spring had arrived, the new frocks were as plentiful and colorful as budding tulips.

"Will we ever have pretty dresses like they wear?" Libby asked Maria as they approached the school grounds.

"If the mill would pay Papa a decent wage you might," Curt put in.

Maria knew that Curt was partly right. Papa put in such long hours and worked very hard. But instead of getting more pay, sometimes his wages were actually cut back. "Pretty dresses aren't all that important," Maria told her younger sister. "Some of those girls in the nicest dresses wouldn't make very good friends."

Libby adjusted her lunch bucket on her arm to a more comfortable position. "I suppose that's true," she agreed with a nod. "But I'd still be a nice person even if I had a million pretty dresses."

Maria looked down at her little sister's cute face with the turned-up nose and tight clusters of chestnut curls beneath the straw hat. She didn't doubt that Libby could do exactly as she said.

Papa's union meetings were held at night. They moved from place to place so the meetings would not be detected by the mill's management. Two days after the Ludlow incident was reported, Papa arrived home late from one of the meetings.

"I am hereby the secretary of the Mill Workers' Union of Minneapolis," he announced.

No one could miss the note of pride in his voice. Mama put her arms around him and congratulated him. Maria and Libby did likewise, and Thomas shook Papa's hand. But Curt just sat at the kitchen table, staring blankly ahead.

"Papa, will this be like Ludlow?" he asked. "Will the army men come and kill us?"

CHAPTER 5
The Suffrage Squad

"Papa's not going on strike," Maria told her little brother. "The men are organizing, not striking."

"But once they're organized, they *might* strike," Curt said.

Maria knew Curt was only saying what they were all thinking. Even Mama's eyes reflected concern.

"Is that right?" Libby wanted to know. "Will you go on strike, Papa?"

"Curt is partly right." Papa gave Libby a pat.

"The Scripture says not to be afraid of evil tidings," Mama told them. "Sit down, Franz. I'll get the coffee. Your supper's in the warming oven."

Papa hung his hat by the door and went to the sink to wash. He'd gone straight to the meeting from work, and the flour was still sprinkled through his dark curls.

After Papa had blessed his food and was eating, he said, "Your question is not forgotten, Curt, but this is not like Ludlow. The mine at Ludlow is owned by the Rockefeller family, who are much more influential in government than the flour mill owners in our city. The other difference is that the strikers there live in company houses, and we do not.

"However," he added, as he took another potato pancake from the platter Mama set before him, "I won't try to tell you there is no danger. No matter where in the country it is, no matter what kind of company, it seems that management constantly fears organized labor unions."

"Why is that, Papa?" Curt wanted to know.

43

"Great profits there are to be raked in when workers are paid meager wages," Papa explained. He poured a little of his hot coffee into his saucer and blew on it, then drank it from the saucer in the manner of all his German relatives. "More and greater factories they build, yet pay workers less, and thereby they become millionaires."

Curt shook his head. "All because of money." He paused a minute. "That's why when I grow up, I'm going out West and work on a ranch. I'll spend every day in the saddle out where no one can bother me. I'll never come back to a city full of factories."

Thomas grinned. "You'll miss your books, Curt."

"That's what you think," Curt said. "I'll have two books in my saddlebags at all times. It's easy to ride and read at the same time. At night I'll read by the light of my campfire."

"Franz," Mama said quietly, "how soon will the mill owners learn about the labor union election?"

Papa gave a shrug. "Word spreads quickly. Even when we try to be as secretive as possible."

" 'He that dwelleth in the secret place of the most High—' " Libby began reciting the Ninety-first Psalm.

" 'Shall abide under the shadow of the Almighty,' " Thomas completed the line.

"Bring the Bible, Libby," Papa told her. "Let's read the entire psalm together."

As Papa read about not being afraid of the terror by night nor the arrow by day, the entire family seemed comforted.

"God is our protector," Papa said as he closed the Bible. "As we do what we know to be right, we trust Him to deliver us from trouble, just as the psalm promises."

"There's a new organization at the high school," Thomas said to Maria the next day after school. "They call it the Junior Mobile Suffrage Squad."

Maria was in the kitchen cutting up cabbage to cook for supper. She almost dropped the knife at his words. "A suffrage group right there at Central High School?"

"Right there at Central. The president of the squad is a girl named SueEllen Jones. I thought perhaps you could talk to her about organizing a group at Washington Elementary."

"Will the squad take part in the suffrage parade on May 2?"

"That's the whole purpose," he replied, flashing his grin.

Aunt Josephine had told them about the upcoming parade to take place in the city, and Maria had already told her aunt that she wanted to take part. But to help organize girls from her own school—that would be even better.

Maria turned back to the cutting block and finished cutting the cabbage. "How well do you know SueEllen Jones? How can I meet her?"

"I don't know her personally, but I'd imagine Aunt Josephine does."

"Oh, Thomas, you're so smart."

"That's what I keep trying to tell you," he said with a chuckle.

"What do you keep telling Maria?" Curt asked as he came in from playing.

"How smart I am," Thomas replied, making Curt groan. Turning back to Maria, Thomas said, "Why don't you go to Mrs. Braun's and telephone Aunt Josephine? Ask her to set up a meeting. She'll probably be glad you thought of it."

Maria scooped up the cut cabbage and dropped it into the boiling beef broth. "But I didn't think of it."

"What difference does that make? Go call."

Maria put a lid on the kettle, pulled off her apron, and hung it on the hook by the stove. "Watch the broth and don't let it boil over. I'll be back in a minute."

As she started to go out the back door, she noticed that Curt was holding a wooden box. He was turning it over and studying it closely.

"What do you have there?" she asked. "That looks like a camera." She stepped closer and watched as Curt opened the front and a bellows and square lens folded out. "It *is* a camera. Where'd you get it?"

Curt set it on the kitchen table so they could get a better look. "Tony found it at the dump. I traded him my slingshot, my Jew's harp, and three of my best shooters for it. He said he didn't have any use for it."

Thomas came now and touched the wooden frame. "That's a Speed Graphic," he said. "Curt, this is a real press camera. The kind the newsmen use."

"Honest?" Curt's eyes grew wide.

"Honest. It may have been stolen. Or lost."

Curt shook his head. "I don't think Tony would lie to me."

"I don't, either," Thomas agreed. "It's true he may have found it at the dump, but it still may have been stolen."

All the air went out of Curt. He sat down at the table. "You think I can't keep it then?"

"Let's let Papa decide," Maria suggested. Just then the broth started to boil over, making the flame on the gas stove spit and sizzle. "Oh no!" She lifted the lid and stirred the cabbage, then turned the flame a little lower.

"Maria," Thomas said, "hurry and make your call. I won't know what to do if it boils over again."

"Just stir it," she said as she hurried out the back door.

Thomas was right. Aunt Josephine did know SueEllen Jones, as well as SueEllen's mother. Aunt Josephine thought it was a great idea for Maria and SueEllen to meet. A time was set for Friday after school. Maria would take the trolley to the Andersons' home.

"Remember," Maria told her aunt, "I haven't asked Mama yet. Thomas just now told me about SueEllen and the suffrage squad."

"Your Mama won't mind. Just leave her to me," Aunt Josephine said with a smile in her voice.

When Maria hooked the receiver back in its place, Mrs. Braun waggled her finger and said, "Now, Maria Schmidt, you should have nutting to do with der vimmen what vant to vote. Nonsense it is about the vimmen and voting. My Johann says so."

"Well, my papa believes that women *should* vote," Maria said as she went out Mrs. Braun's back door.

As she ran back across the yard to her own house, she wished more than ever that they had their very own telephone. Mrs. Braun was such a busybody.

CHAPTER 6
Marching for the Vote

Papa said they would place an advertisement in the classified section of the newspaper to see if anyone had had a camera lost or stolen. "We'll run it twice," he told Curt. "If no one claims the camera within two weeks, then by all rights it is yours."

Curt was quiet, but the whole family could read his face. He was hoping and praying no one would respond. And no one did.

The next step was to see if the camera really worked. Thomas took it to a friend of his who worked in the darkroom at the *Tribune*. The young man, Coleman Wright, said it needed repairs but that it could be fixed. Coleman took Curt to a camera shop downtown, and together they found what was needed and how to fix it.

The next thing the family knew, Curt was spending time at Carnegie Library, checking out books on photography and asking Papa if he could turn the backyard shed into a darkroom to develop photos.

The meeting at Aunt Josephine's house was a pleasant surprise for Maria. She'd feared SueEllen Jones might be like Cathy and Evelyn, who walked through life with their noses in the air. But SueEllen, a senior at Central, was a practical, straightforward girl who was bent on a mission. That mission was to do as much as she could for the suffrage movement.

When Maria met her, SueEllen was dressed in a fitted blue serge jacket that matched her skirt perfectly. Her hat was not at all fussy. Her mother wore a few more tucks and ruffles, and her hat was banded in cute little ostrich tips, but she was equally given to the same mission.

SueEllen seemed pleased that Maria wanted to be involved, but she did give a warning. "Remember that elementary students are still under the influence of their parents—more so than high schoolers." Although SueEllen was sitting on the softest chair in Aunt Josephine's immaculate parlor, she sat on the edge of the seat with her back ramrod straight.

"My suggestion," she went on, "is for you to approach seventh- and eighth-graders only."

Aunt Josephine and Mrs. Jones nodded their agreement. Then Aunt Josephine explained to Maria how the parade idea had come about because of the successful suffrage parade held in Washington, D.C., on the eve of President Woodrow Wilson's inauguration.

"It was so effective that the women wanted to pattern other demonstrations after it." Aunt Josephine paused to take a sip of tea from her china cup. "On May 2 parades will be held in more than a thousand towns and cities in at least thirty-five states."

Maria tried to imagine parades going on all over the nation, rather like the Fourth of July.

"Some people try to tell us that to march is unladylike," SueEllen said, "but that's what they used to say about women attending college. It simply isn't true anymore."

An excited tingle traveled up Maria's back and made her shiver. This is exactly what she'd been trying to say—that she could do anything any boy could do. And that certainly included marching, and demonstrating, *and* voting.

SueEllen armed Maria with a ledger book where she could log the names of those who agreed to take part in the parade. Flyers told details of where the marchers would gather, what time to report, and of course the purpose of the demonstration.

On Monday morning, Maria began her work out on the playground before the first bell. She was able to speak to several eighth-grade girls before anyone knew what she was up to.

There'd already been newspaper articles on the upcoming event, so many students were aware of the parade. But few of the girls had considered that they could take a stand along with the adults. Maria helped change that.

Just when Maria was becoming comfortable talking with the girls about the parade, Charles came up and started yelling so that everyone around him could hear.

"Women ain't supposed to vote," he railed. "They don't know nothing about politics and don't need to know nothing about politics. Next thing you know, women'll be wanting to take up a gun and go to war."

Several students bunched up, curious as to what was going on. Maria felt her face flushing.

"What's up?" one boy asked.

"Aw, Miss Schmidt here is trying to round up more females for that silly march. Women marching!" Charles spat out the words. "It just ain't natural."

"Real ladies don't need to vote. That's what my mother and father both say." Cathy had moved to the front of the crowd. She was dressed in a pale pink dress with pure white stockings and a large pink hair bow holding her curls back from her face. "A lady serves her country in homemaking and in bearing and rearing children," she said. "No man can do that."

Maria turned about to face Cathy. "It's not enough to prepare children for the world." She remembered something Aunt Josephine had once said. "We must have a hand in preparing the world for our children. The best community is where men and women work together for solutions to the problems."

Some of the girls in the crowd clapped their hands. "Good speech, Maria," said an eighth-grader named Abigail Pittman. "Put my name down."

"Me, too," said another.

"I don't know if my papa'll let me come, but put my name down anyway," came another voice. "My heart will be with the parade even if I can't march."

"This is silly," Cathy stated coolly. "Come on," she said to anyone who'd listen. "There are better things to do than stand around here."

The girls who set great store by what Cathy said followed her. Maria was glad to see them go. By the time the bell rang, she had nine names in her ledger book. As they lined up to go into their respective classrooms, she happened to look over and see Torvald Ueland watching her. He smiled. The quiet boy who seldom said much of anything had smiled at her. She smiled back, and then it was time to go in.

At supper that evening, Maria told of the events of the morning. "I'm proud of you, Maria," Thomas said. "There'll always be those who oppose new ideas. Just ignore them."

As they talked about the day, Mama was quieter than usual. At last, she said, "I'm proud of you, too, Maria. Listening to you has made me rethink what Josephine said about needing women in the workplace to join the ranks. Perhaps I'll hand out those flyers for her after all."

Maria jumped up from her place and ran to Mama's side. Throwing her arms about Mama's neck, she said, "You mean it, Mama? You'll help, too? That's wonderful!"

"Gracious me," Mama said, taken aback by Maria's response. "I'm pleased you approve. Now sit down and finish your dinner."

Turning to Papa, Maria said, "Papa, will you join in the parade, as well?"

Papa thought a minute. A smile played at the corners of his mouth. "Mmm. I'm not sure. Is this a conspiracy against me? What with my wife and daughter and my sister-in-law all in cahoots. . ."

"Both daughters," Libby said. "If Maria's in the parade, so am I."

"And I've agreed to help with one of the floats," Thomas said.

Papa laughed. Spreading his big, strong hands, he said, "What chance does a man have? A marcher I will be on the second day of May."

Just then, Curt spoke up. "I don't have to march, do I?"

Curt never liked to be the center of attention. He was a hard worker and absolutely dependable, but he preferred to stay in the shadows.

"Of course you don't *have* to," Mama replied. "Only if you want to. After all, that's what this is about—giving people choices."

Curt thought for a moment. "I'll be along the sidewalk with my new camera."

Papa reached over to give Curt's shoulder an affectionate pat. "A very good idea, son. A good idea indeed."

On the morning of May 2, when the Schmidts arrived at the parade starting point near Second Avenue, Maria stared in awe at the vast crowd. Hundreds and hundreds of women—all nationalities, all ages, and from all economic backgrounds—filled the area. A group of Scandinavian women were dressed in their native costumes with stiffly starched white aprons and red vests embroidered in bright colors. All were gathered for the same purpose, to speak out in favor of giving women the vote.

Maria was terribly proud that both her mama and papa were involved in this famous parade. Mama was able to quickly locate Aunt Josephine. That was when they learned Mama was to lead the group of working women. Papa beamed when he heard it. Aunt Josephine directed Papa to the men's section, which was larger than Maria had expected it to be.

After that, Maria and Libby were taken to the student section, and Thomas went off to help with one of the high school floats. In spite of the mass of people, there was perfect order.

Maria had read the instructions in the flyer of what they were to do. Now SueEllen Jones stood up on a soapbox to repeat the instructions one more time.

"Keep your heads up," she instructed, "your eyes in front of you, and walk in dignity and in silence. No matter what is said or done from the sidelines, continue walking in silence. Be very careful not to respond or reply to any actions or comments."

Through the crowd of students, Maria saw Abigail. Maria smiled and waved, and Abigail waved back. Someone handed Maria a stick with a sign that read WOMEN SHOULD VOTE. Libby was given a small American flag to wave.

It was time to begin. A hushed silence fell over the crowd of nearly two thousand marchers. A strong solemn drum roll sounded from somewhere in the front, and the giant mass of people moved slowly but steadily down Second Avenue. Maria thought it would be easy to keep her eyes in front of her, but it wasn't. It took all her willpower not to look over and see the crowds of onlookers filling up the broad sidewalks on either side of the street.

A feeling of pride welled up inside her. History was being made on this street, and she was part of it. The parade moved in an orderly fashion to Fourth Street, where they turned and followed Fourth to Nicollet Street. Along Fourth, the crowds were denser, and the hecklers were out in full force. As the hoots, boos, and insults began to fly, Maria felt Libby move closer to her side.

"Wave your flag," Maria whispered to her little sister.

Bravely, Libby raised her flag higher, and Maria did the same with her sign. When they came to Nicollet and turned the corner, she saw a gang of boys. One of them was Charles Briggs. Her breath caught in her throat. They were throwing tomatoes at the marchers.

Maria was glad she was on the outside where she could protect Libby. She saw one of the overripe tomatoes fly toward a woman in the section ahead of them, and she heard the splat as it made a direct hit. The boys hooted and cheered. Maria wondered why the police didn't stop them.

As they drew near that corner, she heard Charles yell, "Here's one for you, Maria Schmidt. Go back to the kitchen where you belong."

Maria did not duck or dodge as the tomato came flying right at her. But it sailed in front of her and hit Libby, who let out a yelp. Maria wished it had hit her instead of her sister. Maria wouldn't have let out one little peep. Now she looked down at Libby. The red had splattered on the girl's blue church dress and was dripping down on her white stockings. The tomato was rotten, and the stench was over-powering in the warm sunshine.

Maria wanted to wring Charles's neck. In a loud whisper, she said to Libby, "Lift your flag higher and keep on marching." And Libby did just that!

CHAPTER 7
Curt's Darkroom

When the parade ended at the courthouse, many of the students fussed over Libby and commended her for being so brave. Several produced handkerchiefs and helped wipe off the remains of the tomato, wrinkling their noses at the awful smell.

"My Sunday dress is all stained." Libby was near tears.

Libby was so fussy about her clothes. "Don't worry, Libby," Maria assured her. "Mama can make it come out. She gets the grass stains out of Curt's knickers, doesn't she?"

Now it was time for speeches. Maria kept tight hold of Libby's hand as they listened to the women speak from the podium set up in the street in front of the courthouse. One of the speakers was Mrs. Clara Ueland herself—the one who had organized the entire event. Because of the pressing crowd, Maria didn't have a very good view of the stand, but she could hear the rousing words.

Later in the program, State Senator Ole Sageng stepped to the speaker's lectern. Maria had heard of this senator who was an avid supporter of the suffrage movement. She hung on every word of his speech, which he closed with these words:

It is true, a woman's highest duty is to her home, but that is just as true of man. But what an absolutely crazy and absurd proposition would it not be to argue that he would be a better father and a more loyal husband if we take away from him the right to vote.

57

*American manhood would resent as an insult any serious mention
of such a theory. It is just as much an insult to American woman-
hood to say that giving her the full right of citizenship will inter-
fere with a mother's devotion to her children and her home.*

A deafening cheer went up from the crowd. The marchers held
their flags and signs high and waved them back and forth and cheered
and cheered. Maria yelled until she was hoarse. This man certainly
had the right idea about women and their roles in society.

The next day, an article in the *Journal* gave a favorable report on the
parade. "It was not what the majority of people had expected," the paper
read. "Minneapolis learned by practical demonstration that those who
ask the ballot for women are distinctly not a bevy of hopeless spinsters,
unhappily married women, and persons who have nothing else to do."

The *Tribune's* quotes were equally as positive. Maria clipped the
articles and put them in her scrapbook. She never wanted to forget
that she had had a part in all this.

The backyard shed was now the official darkroom for Curt and his
photography endeavors. Coleman Wright came over several times to
help teach Curt how to develop the photos. Coleman was an unas-
suming young man not much older than Thomas. He'd quit school to
work at the newspaper in order to support his widowed mother. Maria
thought him very kind to take the time to help a little boy like Curt.

Coleman and Thomas ran a long electrical cord from the house
and rigged up a light in the shed. With Coleman's clear instructions,
everything came together quickly.

Curt's first picture-taking adventure was a dismal failure. The
heavy, bulky camera was difficult for a ten year old to handle. At first
Curt was crestfallen. The photos were blurred, and in some there were

people with no heads. He'd been unable to focus correctly.

"I thought all you had to do was point it and shoot," he said in a small voice.

"I think that's a Kodak Brownie," Thomas said.

Coleman suggested that he and Thomas make a tripod that folded so Curt could carry it around with him. It was exactly what Curt needed. Thomas even chipped in some of his earnings from the newspaper route to help Curt purchase chemicals and other supplies.

Seeing Curt's need for extra money gave Maria an idea. "If I were to help you and Thomas with the paper route, you could expand your route," she said when she was alone with Curt. She figured after she sold Curt on the idea, she'd have an easier time presenting it to Mama.

"Since they refuse to give a girl a route, you and Thomas can just ask for your routes to be expanded and I'll help throw. Why," she added as she warmed up to the idea, "I could even sew a canvas bag to carry the papers in. I'd be more than happy to share whatever I make with you. Then you could buy more supplies for your darkroom."

Curt was quiet, but she could tell he was thinking about it. That's all she needed now—for him to think about it. "You can tell me later what you decide," she told him.

Although earning money would be nice, it wasn't the money Maria was after; it was the principle of the thing. To her way of thinking, it was wrong not to allow girls to have their own routes, and this was one way to fight that injustice.

⁓

For days after the parade, Charles Briggs had a heyday making rude comments to Maria about tomatoes. "Had any ripe tomatoes lately?" he taunted. "I hear they're delicious!" Or, "How does your little sister like the color red?" Evelyn and Cathy always seemed to be nearby and twittered their high-pitched giggles. Maria did her best to ignore them.

While she had to put up with Charles's nonsense because of the parade, several of the eighth-grade girls, especially Abigail, treated her with new respect. Abigail invited Maria to sit with them at lunch. Even though the school term was nearly over and these girls would be in high school next year, Maria enjoyed the temporary diversion.

She also enjoyed the warm spring evenings spent playing outdoors with Lloyd and Joanne when Maria's family visited the Andersons' home. Uncle Robert's place had a spacious lawn with cropped grass in which they could run and play. Even Thomas lent a hand helping the younger ones play games of tag, statues, and hide-and-seek.

Libby joined in with hide-and-seek, but she wouldn't hide in any places that might get her dress dirty. And when they threw each other around to play statues, she asked Thomas not to throw her so hard that she landed in the grass.

"I'm not getting any grass stains on this dress," she stated flatly.

Aunt Josephine let them play until almost dusk. She trusted her two children to stay outdoors longer when the older cousins were around to watch them.

One evening, the grown-ups had just finished several games of whist when Aunt Josephine called them all inside to cool off with glasses of sarsaparilla. The windows of the parlor were open, and the May breeze caught the heavy lace curtains and billowed them gently. Uncle Robert had the Victrola cranked up. His favorite song was playing and he sang along:

We were sailing along on Moonlight Bay.
I could hear the voices singing, they seemed to say,
You have stolen my heart, now don't go 'way
As we sang love's old sweet song on Moonlight Bay.

When the song was finished, Uncle Robert moved the needle and played it again. It was a melancholy melody that made Maria feel all hazy and soft inside.

"Maria," Aunt Josephine said, jerking Maria out of her dreamy state, "I was just telling your mama that the suffrage association is making plans to set up a big tent at the state fair in July."

Maria was all ears. "Yes, ma'am?"

"I wondered if you'd like to work at the tent. There'd be ever so many things you could do."

Maria had seated herself on the floor next to one of the open windows. Wisps of hair had escaped from her braids and were clinging to her damp face. She pushed them back. A couple of times when she was alone in her room, she'd tried to put her hair up like Mama did, but it was all slick and slithery and just slid back down again. Of course she didn't use the curling iron like Mama did. But what was the use of so much bother? She didn't care if her hair was all up in a fussy do anyhow.

"What things might I be doing?" she wanted to know.

Aunt Josephine smiled. "The purpose of having the tent is to recruit hundreds of new volunteers and to educate the public about our cause. We'll do that with signs, packets of literature, and of course plenty of ice-cold lemonade and flavored ices. We may even show a flicker that has to do with women's suffrage."

Curt looked up with interest. He loved the flickers.

If Aunt Josephine had already talked to Mama, then permission must have already been given. "I'd love to help, Aunt Josephine," Maria replied. "Put me down as a volunteer."

Aunt Josephine pulled out a small notebook from the nearby table. "Which days can you help?"

"Every day, all day long will be fine with me."

"Don't forget it'll be powerful hot on the fairgrounds in July," Libby reminded her older sister.

"I can handle the heat," Maria shot back. Just as quickly, she was sorry for being so brusque. She knew Libby didn't mean anything by it.

"Libby's right." Aunt Josephine took her pencil and scribbled a note or two. "I'll put you down for all four days, but we'll alternate afternoons and evenings. If you feel like doing more, you may. How's that?"

"Fine. Thank you for asking me." Maria's heart was tripping double-time at the thought. This wouldn't be like a parade where she became swallowed up in the crowd. At the fair, she'd be shoulder-to-shoulder with the key women who worked with the city's suffrage movement. Suddenly July seemed a long way off.

To Mama, Aunt Josephine said, "Clara asked that you attend our next meeting, Christine, so you can assess the strength of our working women's contingency. It's to be held at the Ueland home early next Saturday evening. Will you go?"

"Oh, Josephine," Mama said with a sigh. "I don't know. Can't they get that information from someone else?"

Maria knew Mama never liked to be away from home on her off-hours. Work already kept her away much more than she wanted to be. And Maria wondered if Mama would fit in at the Uelands'. After all, the Uelands were terribly wealthy.

"Just this one time," Aunt Josephine said. "Your input is as vital as any other person's. Several of us are driving our automobiles out to the Uelands. I can pick you up and drop you off again when it's over. It's only four miles west of town."

Glancing over at Papa, Maria noted that he was allowing Mama to make the decision. He was good like that. He gave Mama leave to make a good many of her own decisions—unlike their neighbor, Johann Braun. Mrs. Braun could hardly breathe without her husband telling her when and how deep.

"I suppose just this once," Mama answered. "But I can't devote much more time to the cause, Josephine. Truly I can't."

Aunt Josephine smiled and made more notes in her little book.

CHAPTER 8

Maria, the Newsboy

With obvious reluctance, Mama had gone with Aunt Josephine to the meeting at the Uelands' home. When Mama returned, Libby was itching to know all about what the house looked like. But Mama was noncommittal. Comments like "It was a nice house" and "Mrs. Ueland is a nice lady" told them very little.

Even Maria was a little curious. She'd never been inside a rich person's house before. She knew she wouldn't want to, either. That is, unless she were rich as well.

The next day, Maria, Curt, and Thomas decided to approach Mama about the plan to have Maria help with the newspaper route during the summer.

"But, Maria, I need you here to keep an eye on Libby," Mama protested.

"I'm almost nine," Libby replied. "When Maria was nine, you thought she was old enough to take care of me."

Mama chuckled because Libby was exactly right. "But throwing papers is so unladylike," she said. "I'd hoped you could hire out this summer as a mother's helper to some family in a nearby neighborhood."

"She could still do that in the afternoons," Thomas suggested.

"Yes, I could," Maria echoed.

"With Maria's help," Curt put in, "Thomas and I can take one-half again as much territory, Mama. That's quite a bit."

Mama looked from one child to another. She smiled. "All right. You may try out this plan. But if any circumstances should cause me to change my mind, I reserve the right to do so."

"I'm sure there won't be." Maria beamed with anticipation.

The week before school was out marked the beginning of Maria's new job. She got up each morning at the same time the boys did, donned an old pair of Thomas's knickers, and pushed her blond braids up into one of the boy's caps. The knickers now stayed in a drawer in the bureau in the girls' room—a definite victory in Maria's mind!

At the newspaper office, she hung back so that the adults wouldn't notice her. As soon as the bundles of papers were handed out, she and Curt and Thomas sat down in the alley and folded them. Then they loaded their bags.

Within a couple days, Maria knew the names of most of the newsboys.

"Yer sister's quite a sport," Tony said to Thomas one morning. "Ain't many girls'd wanna do tough chores like throwing papers. 'Specially so early in the morning. Most dames just wanna lay around and sleep late."

Maria wasn't sure what Tony knew about "most dames," but she glowed at his left-handed compliment. After the other boys had gone off with their papers, she mentioned to Thomas that she'd like to bring along a few biscuits for them each morning.

"Be careful how you do that," he warned. "They may be orphans, but they're plenty proud of being on their own. You don't want it to smack of some charity deal. That wouldn't set well at all."

Maria would have to think about that. Perhaps helping these boys wasn't going to be as easy as she'd thought. Thomas handed her bag to her and helped her adjust the strap. She'd learned to fold an old cloth and place it beneath the strap so it wouldn't cut into her shoulder quite so much.

"Why aren't they in the orphanage?" she asked.

Thomas shrugged. "Only so much room in an orphanage. You've never seen the Bohemian Flats. There're so many poor little kids down there, a hundred orphanages couldn't hold them all."

The Flats were the lowlands bordering the Mississippi River where poor immigrants often ended up. The houses were built from tarpaper, tin, and scraps of lumber.

"How could I have ever seen the Flats?" Maria said sharply. "I'm not even allowed to go to the dump."

Thomas shot her his lopsided grin. "Believe me, Maria, the Flats are a lot worse than the dump and more dangerous to boot."

"Someone should go in there and help those people," she said softly, almost to herself.

One morning Tony and Liver Lid both had black eyes and cut lips. It seemed they'd gotten in a scrap with the newsboys from the *Journal*. There was plenty of bad blood between the archrivals.

"You'd think the newsboys would all stick together instead of fighting," Maria said as she walked between her brothers on their way to their routes.

"Since I've never lived alone on the streets, I wouldn't know," Thomas replied. "What I do know is that they're used to fighting for everything and anything they get. Even space on a street corner."

Maria thought about that. Children having to fight to earn a few coins to be able to eat each day. . . It just wasn't right. Then there were all those rich people, like the ones who owned Northwest Consolidated, where Papa worked. Rich people like Evelyn's and Cathy's parents. People like that could buy food for these boys with the money they spent just on a year's worth of collar stays. Something wasn't right.

The newspapers said that the summer of 1914 was the hottest one in over a decade. No one needed to read about it to know it. The night of the elementary school graduation at the end of May had been stifling, and the weather just grew hotter for weeks.

The small bedrooms up under the eaves of the Schmidt house were like ovens. At supper one evening, Mama wondered aloud if they should purchase electric fans and put them in the upstairs windows.

Thomas shook his head. "No need to do that, Mama," he said. "They would only blow hot air. We'll just come down and sleep in the parlor each night."

"Or out in the yard," Curt said, his eyes lighting up. "Like cowboys out on the range."

The week after they gave up sleeping in the hot upstairs, the family celebrated Curt's birthday. He was now eleven. Papa surprised him by announcing that the whole family would go to a cowboy motion picture show. Mama didn't care much for the flickers, but this was a special occasion.

Libby made them promise to go to a moving picture show starring Mary Pickford on her birthday. Mama said they would see. Libby now had a magazine picture of Miss Pickford fastened to their bedroom wall with straight pins. Mama said no one should paint their lips so dark as movie actresses did. But with her long blond curls, Mary Pickford looked like a little girl.

The electric lights of the marquee of the Bijou motion picture theater blinked and sparkled as the six members of the Schmidt family walked down the sidewalk. Since it was Curt's birthday, the children chose to wear last year's school clothes. Even after just a few weeks of going barefooted, Maria's feet rebelled against wearing shoes. Her high-top button shoes squeezed her feet like a pair of vises.

A display case outside the theater held large show bills of coming attractions. Libby was immediately drawn to the bill that said MARY PICKFORD STARRING IN *TESS OF THE STORM COUNTRY*. She stared at the picture with a dreamy look in her eyes. Another bill blared out the words SPECIAL TODAY! It pictured a cowboy in chaps, spurs, and a ten-gallon hat. TOM MIX STARRING IN *WINDS IN THE HIGH SIERRAS*!

Papa paid for the tickets, and they went inside. He removed his hat and nudged the boys to remove their caps. They walked through the lobby, and Papa held back the crimson velvet curtains that hung at the entrance to allow them to go in. They found seats, and within a few minutes the lights dimmed and flickering light lit up the screen. Suddenly the title of the motion picture and the names of the people who starred in it flashed before them. Tom Mix's name was in big letters.

Maria had never seen so much movement go so fast. Men on horseback raised clouds of dust. Indians rode, waving bows and tomahawks in the air. A train raced along the tracks and went hurtling off a cliff. It was as though she could taste the dust and hear the crash. Between scenes, words appeared on the screen to describe the action or tell what the actors and actresses were saying.

All the time the flicker was showing, a man played loud music on a piano down front. He played fast lilting music in the action scenes and slower melodies when Tom Mix was talking to the pretty heroine. Every time Tom Mix talked to the pretty lady, she fluttered her eyelashes. The part Maria didn't like was when the heroine fainted from fright. Maria knew she would certainly never do such a thing.

When they came outside into the evening air, they were all blinking and struggling to get their eyes adjusted to the light. "One would think motion pictures could ruin the eyes of our children if they watched them for very long," Mama said.

Maria was wondering what it would be like to ride a horse fast and free across the prairie, and she knew Curt was thinking the same thing. What fun that would be. Perhaps Curt had a good idea about becoming a cowboy when he grew up.

Papa stopped at a street vendor's wagon and bought each of them a flavored ice. Maria chose lemon because that seemed the coolest. The tart taste on the tiny pieces of chipped ice was wonderful.

Curt was more talkative than usual. He went on about Tom Mix, explaining that the actor had been a real cowboy in Indian Territory, before it became the state of Oklahoma. Curt knew because he read so much.

Maria soaked in the good feeling of all her family being together and the laughter and good-natured teasing they shared. But as they approached their house, they saw the big bulk of Johann Braun standing on the sidewalk. He was gazing at the Schmidt house.

"Wonder what Johann wants?" Papa mused.

"Look," Libby said, pointing. "The window in our front door has been broken."

Mama's hand flew to her mouth to stifle a gasp.

"Now, now. Probably nothing to worry about." Papa put his arm about Mama's shoulders. "Evening, Mr. Braun," Papa called out. "What's happened here?"

"Ya, Franz Schmidt," the big man answered. "About time for you to be home. Look here. Men drive by in der fancy motorcar and throw something at your front door. I told the missus, 'It's the labor union mess, I betcha.' "

"Now don't jump to conclusions," Papa said.

"Rumors we hear all the time about you being a union officer," the beefy man went on. Though Mr. Braun was getting a little stooped and gray on the head, he was still a force to contend with. "Better to stay with fellow Germans than to join the union."

"There are plenty of Germans in our union," Papa replied gently.

Thomas and Curt had hurried inside the house. Now they came out. Thomas held a large rock wrapped in paper. Papa took the rock, untied the string, and opened the crumpled paper. The note said: "Leave the union now and your family will be safe."

"Vat did I tell you?" Mr. Braun's ham-sized hands rested on his hips. "This kind of thing we don't need here." He turned on his heel and stomped off.

After the Schmidts went inside, Mama scurried about gathering rags to stuff in the broken glass. Maria grabbed the broom and swept up broken glass from off the floor.

"Boys," Papa said, "go to the hardware store Monday and purchase a new pane. I'll put it in as soon as I come home from work."

Maria could tell Curt was worrying again. "Are you going to resign, Papa?" he asked.

"Of course he's not going to resign," Maria said. "It's important to stand up for what's right, Curt. You know that."

"I know," Curt said softly. "But it's sure scary."

"I'll say," Libby chimed in.

Maria put her arm around Curt's shoulder. "Just pretend they're the bandits trying to rob the payroll on the train and we're the good cowboys."

Papa chuckled. "Sounds like a good idea to me."

After the entryway was tidy once again, Mama brought out a special cake from the pantry. A light fluffy sugar frosting about an inch thick covered the entire thing. Libby helped Mama put in candles and they sang "Happy Birthday" to Curt. Maria sang loud. She wasn't about to let any rock-throwing coward ruin this special celebration.

But that night as she lay in bed with Libby's steady breathing the only noise in their small room, Maria wondered about the broken window. Was it just an empty threat to scare Papa into quitting? Or did they mean business? What might they do to the family of a union officer? She tried to swallow down the brassy taste of fear in her mouth. Perhaps Curt wasn't the only worrier in the family.

CHAPTER 9
Mrs. Clara Ueland

"Look at this," Liver Lid said, waving one of his papers. "This oughta sell real good."

It was a Monday morning, the last week in June. Even in the early morning hours, the air was sticky and warm.

The bundles had just been handed out, and Liver Lid had cut the rope on his bundle with his jackknife to pull out a copy. He liked to practice the calls and coach the younger boys before they reached the sidewalks.

"Let me see." Curt took the paper from his hand and read aloud, " 'Archduke Franz Ferdinand, heir to the throne of the Austro-Hungarian Empire, and wife, Sophie, assassinated in cold blood at Sarajevo.' " He turned to Thomas. "Who's this archduke fellow? And where's Sarajevo?"

"In the Balkans," Thomas told him. "They're always fighting with one another over there. We've studied about the Balkan wars in history. There've been two wars there in the past two years."

"Two wars in two years?" The thought seemed inconceivable to Curt.

"Two," Thomas answered. "Silly, huh?"

"It's not silly to us," Liver Lid said with a wry smile. "Down in the Flats, we have a war almost every night or so. Especially in this heat."

"War, heat, or Archie-dukes," Tony said, "we got a great yell this morning. Let's stop jawing and get moving."

71

In spite of the heat, Maria basked in the slow summer days. Mama never said another word about Maria hiring out as a mother's helper. Perhaps it was because Maria worked hard to be a good help to her own mama. She and Libby kept the house scrubbed clean and had supper ready every evening when Mama came through the door. And they still had time to play outdoors.

Maria now knew every patron on her paper route and didn't need to tag along with her brothers. She was better at throwing, too. When she tossed a folded paper, it landed right on the porch. Or close by. No longer did her papers land in the shrubs.

Mama had purchased flour sacking at Woolworth's Five and Ten Cents Store for making the girls new underthings. Maria set about teaching Libby how to cut out and sew their bloomers and chemises on the treadle machine. Libby could barely reach the treadle and keep the cloth moving through the bouncing needle at the same time, but she kept at it.

"Our underthings might not be lacy and frilly," Maria told Libby, "but they're durable."

To which Libby replied, "I'd rather have lacy and frilly."

The Fourth of July came on Saturday. That meant Mama and Papa would get the day off for sure. As Maria and the boys threw papers that morning, firecrackers were already sounding through the neighborhood. By the time they arrived back at the house, Mama and Libby had a picnic lunch packed in the wicker basket, covered with one of Mama's embroidered tea towels.

Papa carried the basket as they walked downtown for the parade. Curt carried his camera and tripod, and Thomas offered to carry Curt's satchel that contained other camera equipment. Downtown stores were draped in bright red, white, and blue bunting, and the drum-and-bugle corps and fire brigades were decked out in neatly pressed uniforms.

As she stood along the sidewalk, Maria remembered marching down that street herself a couple months ago. Now there were no jeers or rotten tomatoes. Flags waved and cheers sounded as the bands marched by. Maria cheered, too, thankful that she was an American living in a free country. A place where, in spite of rotten tomatoes, they were allowed to assemble and march for what they believed.

Following the parade, the Schmidts rode the trolley to Central Park, where there would be brass bands and fireworks that evening. All Papa's German relatives would be celebrating at one of the large biergartens, and they expected the Schmidts to be there as well.

But Mama had asked Papa if they could forgo the biergarten this time. "After all, we go there nearly every Sunday."

To which Papa replied, "Perhaps you're right, Christine."

Even under the largest shade trees, the air was sweltering. "Must be a hundred and ten in the shade," Thomas said as they spread their lunch out on the grass.

But not even the heat could stop people from having a fine time. Strains of the popular song "After the Ball Is Over" sounded from the bandstand, and people in the crowd joined in singing the lyrics. Anyone who had a Victrola had a recording of the song. At least, that's what Uncle Robert said. He was always singing along to his Victrola.

Curt spent the afternoon taking photographs and could hardly wait to get home to develop them. The most recent ones he'd taken had turned out better. Coleman said he was learning fast.

As Maria and Libby strolled together through the meandering graveled walks, Maria heard someone call out her name. She turned around to see SueEllen Jones.

"Maria Schmidt! I've not seen you since the suffrage parade."

Maria was surprised to be greeted so exuberantly by a high-school graduate. "Hello, SueEllen. Nice to see you."

If SueEllen sensed Maria's discomfort, she didn't let on. She folded down her parasol and turned her attention to Libby. "And here's our girl who bravely took a missile in battle and lived to tell about it," she said with a smile.

"Mama got all the stain out," Libby said, which of course was the most important issue to her. Maria wasn't all that sure that Libby even felt strongly about women voting, but then, she was still young.

"Mamas are good at things like getting stains out," SueEllen said. "I've needed that help many times myself. But not always from a rotten tomato."

"I received your thank-you note after the parade," Maria said. "That was kind of you." Maria certainly hadn't expected to be formally thanked for the recruiting she'd done.

"I appreciated your wanting to join in, Maria. Next year when I attend college, I'll be active in a campus group. It's time to groom younger girls like you to come into the ranks and carry on the work that I must leave behind."

"You're going to college?" The girl had said it in the same tone that Maria would have said, "I'm going to the store for bread."

SueEllen nodded. "Mama and I determined years ago that I would get a good education. Tell me," she said, changing the subject, "are you going to help out at the suffrage tent at the fair?"

"I am. Aunt Josephine has already asked me."

"Wonderful. On which days are you scheduled?"

"I just told her to put me down for every day all day long."

SueEllen laughed. She made Maria feel as though the two of them shared a private joke. "You *are* committed, aren't you?"

"My aunt scheduled me for alternating afternoons and evenings and said I could stay longer if I felt like it."

SueEllen nodded, and the veil on her stylish hat waved a little. "As Mrs. Ueland often says about our best workers, 'We could use a dozen like you.'" SueEllen smiled again and held out a gloved hand. "I'll see you at the fair."

Maria had shoved her gloves in her pocket because she'd been out of Mama's sight and because it was so hot. But she stuck out her bare hand and returned the handshake, only a tad mortified. She didn't think girls should have to mess with frilly hats and hot binding gloves anyway. After all, boys never did.

As she and Libby continued their walk, Libby said, "SueEllen's a nice lady. And she talks to you just like you were grown up, too."

Later Maria thought about SueEllen. The girl wasn't particularly pretty. In fact, she was rather plain. But she'd presented such a pleasant appearance in her pastel summer dress and matching hat and gloves. And she was going to go to *college*. Just like a man would do! As Maria watched the brilliant explosion of fireworks light up the night sky, she puzzled over SueEllen Jones.

A film of gray dust coated everything and everyone in and around the suffrage tent. Even Maria's throat was coated. The large yellow-and-white-striped tent with its open sides fended off the glaring sunlight, but nothing could relieve the stifling heat.

Bright melodies from the merry-go-round calliope floated across the still air, along with the sounds of noisy barkers luring patrons into their various sideshows. Aromas of cotton candy, roasted peanuts, and buttery popcorn added to the festive atmosphere.

The ice wagon made regular stops at the suffrage tent. The huge, shiny, dripping blocks were lifted from the wagon into galvanized tubs by men with metal ice hooks. The women covered them with burlap bags to keep them from melting quickly. With ice picks, they chipped away and prepared cup after cup of lemonade for the passersby. They also had an ice crusher to make cups of flavored ice. The women enjoyed the job of chipping ice since it was the coolest place to be.

On the plank-wood tables were pies the ladies were selling for a nickel a slice, everything from custard to raisin cream to lemon topped with inches-high, light-as-air sugary meringue.

Maria mostly stood outside the tent with an armful of flyers and handed out the literature. Even in her lightweight summer dress, she was soaked in perspiration, but she didn't care. She was working for something she believed in.

Some men glanced at the pamphlets, then threw them on the ground. One man spit on his. Maria watched their behavior and marveled that such uncouth people should be able to vote when the decorous ladies under that tent could not. The thought made her all the more determined. Waiting until the men were gone, she'd retrieve the pamphlets from the dust, wipe them off, and hand them out again. All except for the paper that was spit on. She decided that one was best left alone.

At nightfall, they projected the flicker on a bedsheet strung up in the tent. The charge was two cents per person, but not many people paid to see it. The ladies had to drop down the sides of the tent to show it, or else everyone could just stop by and watch for free. That made it even hotter inside. Who wanted to pay two cents to swelter in a tent when the midway was full of exciting things to do? But nothing fazed the women. Maria heard one say, "We'll know to do something different next time."

Mrs. Ueland swept in and out at various times. Maria watched this woman who was soon to become head of the suffrage association of the entire state—not just the city of Minneapolis. In spite of the heat, she looked cool and calm. Her large hat, trimmed in full rose-colored ostrich plumes, sat at a fashionable tilt on her graying hair, and her dusky rose crepe de chine dress looked like it just came out of Jessica's Ready-to-Wear Fashions in downtown Minneapolis.

At one point, SueEllen Jones explained to Maria that Mrs. Ueland's job during the fair was to coordinate all the efforts. The suffrage leader noted when supplies were low and made sure items were delivered to the tent on time. She also conferred with those who coordinated the workers' schedules. Maria marveled that one person could manage so many details. Surely the president of Northwest Consolidated couldn't have done any better.

Each morning, Maria threw her papers, then changed into her summer dress and took the trolley to the fairgrounds. Aunt Josephine was there off and on, and Mama stayed one evening to help. On the third evening, Maria had the job of bending over the ice tub to chip smaller chunks from the ice blocks for the lemonade. She was thankful for her strong paper-throwing arm. Suddenly, she felt a touch on her shoulder. A pleasant voice behind her said, "Tell me, whose daughter are you?"

Maria turned and found herself face-to-face with Mrs. Ueland. Her first thought was that Mrs. Ueland wouldn't know her mother even if she said her name. Then she remembered that Mama had indeed met Mrs. Ueland at the Uelands' house last spring. But by the time she got her wits about her, Aunt Josephine, who was working at her elbow, spoke up.

"This is my niece, Clara. You met my sister-in-law, Christine Schmidt, before the parade in May. This is Christine's daughter, Maria."

Mrs. Ueland had deep-set eyes and a long, straight nose. She smiled and said, "Schmidt, is it? I could have sworn you were Norwegian, as hard as you're working." She held out her hand. "I'm pleased to meet you, Maria Schmidt."

Nervously, Maria put the dripping ice pick in her other hand, wiped her wet hand on her apron, and returned Mrs. Ueland's handshake. "Pleased to meet you as well," she said as politely as she knew how.

"I've been watching you, Maria. Every time I come by the tent, you've been here doing one task or another. Tell me, does the suffrage movement mean that much to you, or are you just looking for something to do?"

"Oh no, ma'am. I believe with all my heart that we should have the right to vote. I mean *women* should."

Mrs. Ueland laughed. "You were right the first time, Maria. This is for you as well. After all, you'll be grown up and ready to vote before you know it." Someone handed Mrs. Ueland a cup of lemonade, and she thanked the person before taking a long sip.

"Maria," she continued, "every August I conduct a suffrage fundraising garden party at our home in the country. There are a number of preparations that must be made ahead of time."

Maria couldn't imagine why Mrs. Ueland was telling her this. Then to Maria's everlasting shock, the suffrage leader finished by saying, "I need a hard worker to lend me a hand. Would you consider being one of my helpers?"

CHAPTER 10
Beware of the Huns

Maria was sure she'd heard wrong. Why should Mrs. Ueland choose her, of all people?

"Of course, if you'd rather not. . . ," Mrs. Ueland added.

"Oh no, I'd like to. Very much." Maria glanced at Aunt Josephine, who was smiling. "I'd have to ask Mama," she added as an afterthought.

"Of course," Mrs. Ueland said.

"Your mama's sure to say yes," Aunt Josephine put in, still smiling.

"We'd need you to come at least three days ahead of time. We have plenty of rooms in our house, now that my older girls are grown."

"Robert would be pleased to drive her out in our automobile," Aunt Josephine offered.

"Splendid. I'll look forward to having you then." Mrs. Ueland handed her empty cup back to Maria, pulled on her gloves, and turned to go. "Oh, and it won't be all work. There are all sorts of delightful things to do in the country."

After she'd gone, Aunt Josephine said, "Now, Miss Maria, what do you think of that? Looks like your suffrage work for the summer is cut out for you."

Maria was still in shock. Whatever would she do around a whole houseful of rich folk?

Maria was much more comfortable dealing with the newsboys. Tony and Liver Lid treated Maria with the same respect they gave Thomas and Curt. She'd proven herself through the summer. Tony told her one day, "I was flat out sure you'd cave in soon's you got over the new feeling. You're a mighty good sport."

The compliment poured over her like warm honey. Now that they trusted her, she brought apples and raisins and biscuits and whatever else she could grab each morning to share with them. Usually, Tony and Liver Lid turned around and gave it to the littler guys. She admired them for that. They all seemed to watch out for one another.

That is, unless it was the gang from the *Journal*. Then it was war. There was constant bickering over who had rights to what street corners. Liver Lid said the best spots were right at Washington Square where the trolleys stopped to let off the wealthy businessmen who worked in those tall buildings downtown.

The last week in July, the boys were again excited. Great headlines! On the previous day, July 28, Austria had declared war on Serbia. They were shelling the city of Belgrade.

"We'll sell every paper we got," Tony said with a grin.

After supper that night, Papa looked up from reading the German newspapers. Germany was tightly allied with Austria-Hungary, he said. "Now that the Fatherland has built up a stronger navy," Papa went on, "they'll not be afraid to fight."

"Do you mean," Thomas asked, "that Germany may get into this tussle between two small countries like Serbia and Austria just because some old stuffy archduke was assassinated?"

Papa said, "We'll see. But there's much more here than what you call a 'tussle between two small countries.'"

Papa was absolutely right. Headlines the very next Saturday declared that because Russia was building up arms to lend aid to Serbia, Germany had declared war on Russia.

"Think of that," Thomas said as they sat in the alley folding their papers. "Those two big strong countries at war with one another."

"Papa says the Germans can whip the Russkies any day," Curt said. "And the Limeys and Frenchies thrown in for good measure."

"That doesn't mean Papa is in favor of war." Maria quickly came to Papa's defense. "He's just repeating what Uncle Werner and Uncle Heinz are always saying. All they ever talk about is how powerful the kaiser's well-trained *Reichswehr* is. You'd think they were ready to sail over there and join up."

Thomas smiled. "They do get carried away at times. But if we'd been born there, we might feel the same way."

"I'd never be in favor of war," Curt said solemnly. "No matter where I was born."

Sunday afternoon after church, Papa wanted to go to the biergarten to learn what was going on. Most of their German friends had scores of relatives back in Germany and received letters regularly.

That day, the festive gathering was highlighted with more national songs than Maria ever remembered hearing before. The Germans, who loved to sing, sang chorus after chorus as the band played the rousing accompaniment. Many of them proclaimed that the war would be over in three weeks. *Deutschland Über Alles*—"Germany over all," the national anthem promised.

Flyers were handed out giving times and places for meetings of the German-American National Alliance, which met to discuss foreign affairs. Mama didn't favor such meetings, but Maria noticed that Papa folded the flyer and slipped it inside his coat pocket.

The next week things happened so fast hardly any American could keep up. Suddenly, everyone was fighting everyone else in Europe. Thomas said it was like a row of dominoes toppling down one after the other.

Now even Thomas agreed to purchase a copy of the newspaper to bring home and read each day. By the end of the first week in August, the situation had reached gigantic proportions.

France, who was allied with Russia, began to take military action. So on August 3, Germany declared war against the French people. Germany was poised to strike through Belgium in order to attack France.

Britain declared that the tiny country of Belgium was neutral and should remain so. The British government demanded that Germany withdraw from Belgium. When the Germans refused, Britain declared war on Germany. Britain's ally, Japan, sided with Britain.

Papa shook his head as he read the news aloud to the family late one evening. "It's as though the entire world is suddenly at war."

"The whole world?" Curt asked in a serious tone. He shook a dark shock of hair back out of his eyes. "Has the whole world ever been at war before?"

"Never," Papa answered. "Never like this."

Papa attended two of the Alliance meetings, but he returned home solemn and stone-faced. When Mama asked him how the meetings went, he said little. This wasn't like their papa. He usually came home from any German meeting in high spirits and brimming over with news.

"Why has Papa been so quiet?" Curt asked one morning a week after the first news hit. They were walking home from their route.

"He doesn't agree with what the Fatherland is doing," Thomas replied. "Especially since they attacked the defenseless country of Belgium."

"Are they really killing women and little children?" Curt asked.

Thomas nodded. "That's what the reports say."

"But why?" Curt was in total disbelief, and Maria couldn't blame him. It all seemed so strange. Curt looked to Thomas to have all the answers, but this time Thomas could only shrug.

"I don't understand it, Curt," he answered in a quiet voice. "I don't understand it at all."

Libby got her wish. In mid-August on her ninth birthday, the family again attended the flickers together. *Tess of the Storm Country* was the main attraction.

That night, a newsreel showed before the moving picture. Frightening scenes of rows upon rows of goose-stepping German soldiers flashed across the screen. The words on the screen criticized the actions of Kaiser Wilhelm II, Germany's leader. Maria was certain that had it not been Libby's birthday celebration, Papa would have stood and led his family from the theater.

The next week, Maria packed a small satchel with a few things to take to the Uelands' home. Uncle Robert was to pick her up the next morning and take her out. Mama had purchased an end piece of a nice cotton print from a table in the basement of Woolworth's, and together they'd sewn Maria a new dress. Maria didn't think a new dress was necessary for the occasion, but Mama seemed to think it was. The dress was simple but certainly not as worn and faded as Maria's other everyday dress.

That night Papa gathered them all in the parlor to make an announcement. Maria had never seen Papa's face look so grave. He put on his reading glasses and took the Bible into his lap.

"I have something to say to you as my family," he said. "I've prayed and mulled this matter over for several days, but now I feel that no longer do I have a choice. From this day on," he continued, "I will never attend another German Alliance meeting. Nor will I attend a German festival or gathering so long as my fellow Germans condone the barbaric action occurring in the country of Belgium."

Maria sat in stunned disbelief. She looked over at Thomas, but Thomas was staring at Papa. None of them could understand it. Papa not spend time with his own family? This must be much more serious than they'd first thought.

Mama said softly, "Whatever you think best, Franz. We will support you in it."

Papa read Scripture then, and they prayed together. Papa prayed especially that the fighting would quickly come to an end.

The next morning, Curt was doing more reading than folding of the newspapers, when suddenly his eyes grew wide. "Thomas. Maria. Look at this."

"Curt," Thomas said sternly, "it's bad enough you read the front page. Don't be opening up the papers before we get them delivered."

As he spoke, Thomas looked over at the page. Maria peered over his shoulder. A political cartoon pictured an evil-faced German soldier in uniform with hate-filled, wild eyes and hideous fangs for teeth. On his bayonet were the doll-like bodies of children dripping in blood. Beneath the picture was the statement BEWARE OF THE HUNS.

Curt looked up at Thomas. "Am I a Hun?"

"Well, of course you're not," Maria snapped, yanking the paper from his hands and folding it as quickly as she could. "What a silly thing to ask. You're an American just like I am. Just like Thomas is. Like Mama and Papa are. We're all Americans, Curt. Now let's hurry. Uncle Robert will be coming for me in a couple hours."

But for all her bluster, Maria couldn't get the ghastly picture out of her mind.

CHAPTER 11

In the Country

The sixteen-room, three-story Ueland house looked like an oversized farmhouse. It sat behind a row of trees just off the deeply rutted Calhoun Road. While it was large, the house was simply designed. It had a large triple-window dormer jutting from the rooftop, with rounded graceful bay windows beneath that. Maria could see that the wide porch wrapped around two sides. A barn stood a ways from the house, painted a flat barn red. Down a grassy hill from the house lay Calhoun Lake, shimmering in the midday sun.

Maria's insides wouldn't quit rumbling as she wondered what the next three days held for her. Uncle Robert had attempted to make polite conversation along the way, but Maria could hardly talk. The jarring ride on the rutted road hadn't helped any. Now that they'd finally arrived, her mouth was dry as a cotton ball.

Mama had insisted Maria wear her church dress and her good hat for the drive and pack her everyday things in the satchel. Maria didn't see any need for getting gussied up when she was only coming to work, but there was no arguing with Mama.

When the Model T rumbled to a stop, Uncle Robert grabbed her satchel and opened the door to help her out. In a nearby field, workers were assembling makeshift booths. That would obviously be the location of the fund-raising event.

As they stepped up on the porch, the sound of whooping and shouting came from the lake. Maria turned to see two boys playing at the edge of the water—with their shirts unbuttoned! She recognized Torvald and his older brother Rolf. Why, she'd almost forgotten about Torvald. Of course he would be here—how silly of her to have forgotten. Quickly she turned back again, pretending she hadn't seen the flapping shirttails. She could hardly believe such audacity.

As Uncle Robert rapped the brass knocker, he leaned over to her and smiled. "I believe they have on their woolen swim togs beneath the shirts."

Maria felt her face grow bright crimson. The door opened and a young lady in a maid's uniform appeared. "Yes?" she said. "Oh, Dr. Anderson. Did someone call for you? Is the missus ill?"

"This isn't my black bag," he said in his joking tone as he removed his hat. "This belongs to my niece here. Maria's come to help with the fund-raiser."

"Ah, of course. We're pleased to have extra hands about. Couldn't do it all myself, even if I'd a mind to, which I don't. Not in this heat at any rate." The maid stepped back.

"Come in, come in," she said. "Whatever am I thinking? I've not even thought to give me own name, I haven't." She gave a little curtsey as Uncle Robert and Maria stepped into the entryway. "I'm Carolyn, but the folks all call me Carrie and you can, too." Her brogue seemed to lilt along like a gurgling little brook. "Will you be a-staying, Dr. Anderson?"

Uncle Robert shook his head. "I'm only the driver for this mission. I must get back to my office right away." Replacing his hat, he kissed Maria gently on her cheek, bade her good day, and left.

"Mm," Carrie said thoughtfully. "Shall I take you to your room first or take you to see the missus?"

Maria didn't know the answer. But it didn't matter because Carrie was just thinking out loud. "Best take you to the missus. I haven't the faintest notion where she wants you to sleep, I don't."

Maria picked up her satchel and followed Carrie down the hallway into a great center hall with low oak paneling and a red-tile fireplace. A perfect place for a Christmas dinner celebration.

"This here's the library," Carrie said as she moved on down a narrower hall and stood before a closed door. She tapped at the door. "Pardon, Mrs. Ueland. A girl named Maria here to assist with the goings-on."

"Come in," came the answer.

Like the rest of the house, the library was large and spacious but not elaborate or ornate. Everything had a scrubbed, lived-in look. Mrs. Ueland was without hat and gloves, and her dress was a serviceable polished cotton print in pink tones—not at all what Maria thought this woman would wear at home. Now Maria wished more than ever that she wasn't decked out fit to kill.

Mrs. Ueland rose to greet Maria and welcomed her to their home. "As I told you at the fair, we have many extra bedrooms now that our five older children are gone," she said. "You're welcome to any of them. But I should think you'd like Sandra's old room since it faces south. You can see the lake from there and catch the breeze as well."

"That's fine, thank you." Maria had thought she might have to stay with the hired help—wherever it was that the hired help stayed. Later, she learned that the maid and cook lived on the third floor and used a back stairway. The hired man, Herb, had a room in the barn.

"Please make yourself at home in your room," Mrs. Ueland was saying. "As soon as you're comfortable, come back here and we'll talk about the work that's to be done."

Carrie led the way to the upstairs bedroom and then dismissed herself. "You'll be comfy in this here room, missy," she said. "Now I mustn't be standing around like I was addlepated. The missus is kind but doesn't hold with lollygagging about, she doesn't. I'll see you directly."

"Thank you, Carrie." Maria started to extend her hand, but Carrie gave a little curtsey and was gone.

For a moment, Maria stood in the middle of the room and just stared. It was spacious and airy. So much larger than her small room beneath the eaves—and cooler as well. Probably warmer in winter, too. Wallpaper in an ivy and lattice pattern gave the room a cool look, as did the white furniture.

Setting her satchel on the cedar chest at the foot of the bed, she stepped to the window. The browning pasture sloped away from the house toward the sparkling lake, which was surrounded by a thick stand of oaks, maples, and blackjack. The Ueland brothers were in the lake, swimming around like fish.

Turning from the window, she stepped to a dainty vanity table with a cushioned stool in front of it. Maria picked up a small hand-carved ivory jewel box that stood on miniature legs. The artwork was exquisite. Returning it to its place, she ran her fingers over the pale blue satin handkerchief case, the sides of which were covered with plaited satin. On a silver tray were several cut-glass atomizers. One smelled like lily-of-the-valley. *What girl,* she wondered, *would move away from home and leave behind all these lovely things?*

But she'd dallied long enough. What had Carrie said about Mrs. Ueland not holding with lollygagging? Maria changed into her new cotton print, then peered at her reflection in the mirror above the washstand. A few strands of hair had blown loose due to the windy ride with Uncle Robert. She tucked them back into her braids, then washed her dusty face and hands before going back downstairs.

Mrs. Ueland invited her to be seated as they discussed all that was to happen in the next few days. "When the frivolity begins," she said with a wry smile, "it's great fun. But first there is a great deal of hard work."

She nodded toward the back of the house. "You saw the carpenters working. Those are the booths. We'll have a country store where we sell apples, jellies, pickles, and doughnuts. There'll be a white elephant booth with anything and everything for sale—silly things like bears' teeth and a nightcap belonging to someone's grandmother." She chuckled. "Our volunteers have wonderful imaginations."

Maria found herself wondering why she'd been so nervous. Mrs. Ueland was delightful.

Looking at a list on her desk, the woman continued, "There'll be a dishpan band, an onstage skit called 'How the Vote Was Won,' games, and even a few athletic events. Our guests shell out good hard cash for each event, and we raise a great deal of money to push forward with our work."

"Now," she said, looking up from the list, "there's cooking to be done, sewing, and decorating. Some of our volunteers will be on hand at various times in the next few days. You certainly won't be working alone. The boys will help, too. They're down at the lake now taking a quick swim. I allow them time to play and cool off during the day."

She looked at Maria then. "Do you swim?" she asked.

Maria shook her head. She had never had a chance to learn to swim, but it was an exciting thought.

"I didn't suppose so, but at any rate, you can wade in the lake if you'd like. It's wonderfully refreshing. I do it myself from time to time."

Maria studied Mrs. Ueland more closely, straining to imagine this dignified woman wading in the lake.

"Where was I? Oh yes, ladies will be here to help out, and you just join in and do what they tell you. Can you sew?"

"Oh yes, ma'am. I sewed most of this dress I have on."

"Excellent. A nice dress it is. For today, you can help the seamstress work on the buntings. She's in the game room at the rear of the house. Lizzie Higgins is her name. She used to sew all my girls' dresses when they were younger. Not much to do around here anymore, so I only hire her at times like this."

Mrs. Ueland paused then, as though to collect her thoughts. "All right then, you may go. And if you have any questions, feel free to ask."

"Thank you, ma'am," Maria replied.

As she turned to leave, Mrs. Ueland added, "You'll work only during the daytime. After supper your time belongs to you. Torvald and Rolf can show you around."

Then, as though she were sizing Maria up, she added, "The boys have old knickers you can wear to play in. You wouldn't mind, would you?"

"Oh no, ma'am," Maria said. Then realizing how enthusiastic she'd sounded, she added, "That would be fine, thank you."

Mrs. Ueland laughed. "I tend to agree, Maria. Dresses are terrible things for play. My girls always wore their brothers' knickers when they played ball games and such."

The day flew by. Lizzie Higgins was a delightful old lady who could sew a beautiful seam on the treadle machine. She set Maria to pulling basting threads, but later Lizzie let her sew hems as well.

At one point in the afternoon, Torvald came in and politely welcomed Maria and introduced her to Rolf. Rolf, who had the same clear blue eyes and sandy hair as his younger brother, was a year older than Thomas.

"After supper, we'll show you the animals in the barn," Torvald told her. "And the lake, too, if you'd like."

The boys didn't stay long. They said they were helping the carpenters with the booths and had to get back to work. Torvald's kindness left Maria amazed. At school he was so quiet and reserved.

When the workday was finished, Maria was surprised to find she was invited to join the family at their supper table. Attorney Andreas Ueland was a balding man who had a twinkle in his eyes, a smile on his lips, and a heavy Norwegian accent in his voice. Maria found herself listening closely to make out his words. The family laughed and talked together a great deal during the meal.

Attorney Ueland made several jokes about the upcoming event, which would cause the grass to be trampled down and leave more trash and destruction behind than a "herd of wild African elephants," he said. Mrs. Ueland merely laughed. Her husband's jokes hadn't offended her one bit.

The boys were good to their word. Maria was given a boys' blouse and a pair of knickers that fit her perfectly. After she'd changed, the boys showed her all around. At the barn she saw a few chickens, a cow, a driving and riding horse, and a lovely spotted pony. Maria immediately thought of Curt and how he would love this place. Especially the pony.

"Do you ride him?" she asked. The pony was pushing up against the corral fence, and she was able to reach through the fence and pet his nose. It was softer than the velvet on Mama's Sunday hat.

"Sure," Torvald answered. "All the time. Although Rolf here is almost too big for her now. His feet practically drag on the ground."

Maria laughed. Rolf's legs were pretty long and lanky.

"Want to ride?" Rolf asked. "He's tame as a kitten."

"Oh, could I?"

"If you're willing, the pony is willing," Torvald said.

In no time, the pony was saddled and bridled, and Maria was astride the little horse. The boys instructed her in how to guide using the reins, and she rode round and round inside the corral.

Once she had the hang of it, Rolf saddled the horse. The boys rode double and together with Maria rode down through the tall, dry grass in the pasture and around the lake. The sun was setting, sending golden streaks across the water. In the trees, insects were setting up an evening chorus. Maria had never been in such a peaceful place. Perhaps Curt was right about wanting to spend his life out West—out of the city.

CHAPTER 12
The Fund-Raiser

That night up in the room, Maria sat on the window seat and stared out at the stillness and the glittering stars. The sight of the moon on the water made her think of the record on Uncle Robert's Victrola about Moonlight Bay. Only this was Moonlight Lake.

Night sounds filtered up to her window as did the breeze off the lake. It made her feel all soft and dreamy deep down inside, almost like the sweet music of Uncle Robert's favorite song. She was sure she was much too full of exciting new things to ever be able to sleep. But as she lay in the wide, soft bed, tiredness quickly overtook her, and she was asleep in no time.

In the next two days, she did everything from cooking, to cleaning, to decorating the booths. The boys pitched in, not seeming to care whether they were doing women's work. They were as adept in the kitchen as the cook, yet both of them could swing a hammer and hang bunting with ease. They amazed Maria.

The second evening, the three friends played in the shallow edges of the lake. At first, Maria tried not to soak the cuffs of the knickers she was wearing. But the boys insisted it didn't matter. Then to prove it, they began splashing her. She was shocked, but almost by instinct she splashed them back. The war was on.

Soon all three were breathless with hysterical laughter. By the time they went inside, they were soaked. Maria had never had such fun in her entire life. It didn't seem to matter that she wasn't acting like a lady.

Not for a moment did Maria feel out of place during her three-day stay. That is, not until the guests began arriving. She'd conveniently put that out of her mind—the fact that wealthy guests would be swarming over the place.

When she saw Rolf and Torvald in their expensive, custom-tailored suits with stiff, starched collars, Maria felt like disappearing. She'd brought her church dress, of course, but not even her church dress would be appropriate on such an occasion as this.

No one had said a thing about her working during the festivities, so Maria hid up in the haymow of the barn. Since Mrs. Ueland had hired a team of servers, there was nothing for Maria to do. From the haymow she could observe all the comings and goings and yet not be seen. The guests numbered well over three hundred. Maria had never seen so many exquisitely dressed people in one place at one time.

What a crying shame that the cause of women voters has to depend on these arrogant, well-heeled people, Maria thought. Surely there had to be a better way.

Later, she heard noises below the ladder. Thinking it was Herb, the hired hand, she just sat very still. After a moment, Torvald's head appeared through the opening in the floor. "Maria? Ah, I thought you might be up here."

Embarrassed at being caught, she gave a nervous laugh. "It's a better view from up here. Not as likely to get trampled on."

He'd climbed the ladder one-handed, because his other hand was carrying a plate mounded up with goodies—sandwiches, deviled eggs, fruit, and iced cakes with candied fruit on top. "Here's your 'just desserts.' For being a good sport when we splashed you in the lake."

She chuckled in spite of herself. Torvald was up in the haymow now, stepping over a large mound of hay as he came toward her.

"You shouldn't be up here," she told him. "Your suit will get filthy."

He shook his head. "Dusty maybe. Not filthy." He handed her the plate as he folded his long legs and sat down beside her.

"Thank you." The food did look very good. All the aromas had been drifting up from the various booths, and she'd had no supper. She ate a deviled egg, savoring its vinegary tartness.

Torvald watched through the slatted window with her and never did ask her why she was sitting in the haymow. Instead, he told stories about his parents. His mama, he told her, had been reared by a widowed mother who took in sewing. At one time, Clara Ueland, her younger brother, and her mother were forced to live with relatives in a few rooms above a local hardware store.

His papa, too, had lost his father when he was very young and then decided to leave his native Norway and come to America.

"Papa laughs about learning English," Torvald said with a smile. "He still has the little book, *One Hundred Lessons in English,* which cost him three dollars—three dollars he needed desperately just for food. His accent was so pronounced that when he tried some of his first cases as an attorney, people in the courtroom could barely understand him."

Maria finished off the last piece of cake, licking the sweet frosting from her fingers. She pulled her handkerchief from her pocket to wipe them a little cleaner and gazed down at all the people. Then she looked across at the big Ueland house. She mulled over what Torvald had shared with her. Both Mr. and Mrs. Ueland had experienced lack in their younger days, yet somehow in their wealth they'd not forgotten their past.

"I can take you around the back way out of the barn and get you upstairs to your room without anybody seeing you," Torvald said. "If you stay up here until all the guests leave, it'll be nearly dawn."

Maria hadn't thought about that. Uncle Robert would be out to fetch her early the next morning, and she was tired. "Yes, I'd like that."

Taking the plate, Torvald went down the ladder first, then just as he promised, he led her around the way where there were no guests. He tipped his cap and said good night to Maria at the bottom of the maids' stairs. "On the second floor, it opens into the large hallway closet. You'll get your bearings when you enter the hall."

Thanking him again, Maria slipped up the stairs, through the closet, into the hall, and down to her room. *Torvald Ueland,* she thought as she fell asleep that night, *is a terribly nice boy.*

Maria's brothers were glad to have her back home. "Here you talk us into getting extra long routes, then leave us high and dry," Thomas teased. But she loved the teasing. It meant they truly appreciated her work.

All the family wanted to know every detail of her stay, but she hated to tell everything. Mama wouldn't take too kindly to her romping in the lake with knickers on. But she did tell as much as she felt she could, and that was still plenty, because so much had happened. She told Libby about some of the beautiful gowns the ladies wore to the gala fund-raiser event.

It wasn't until after Maria was home again that she realized not one word about the war had been mentioned at the Uelands'. Not at any mealtime conversation nor any other time. It was as though it wasn't happening at all. Yet now that she was home, the boys filled her in on all the details. With tears in his eyes, Curt told about the burning of a priceless old library in the city of Louvain, Belgium.

"Ransacked and burned by the German army," Curt said in a tight little voice. "How could anyone burn books? Any book would be bad enough. But a whole library?"

What Curt didn't say, and what Maria knew he meant, was not just that the library had been burned, but that it had been burned by some of their distant relatives and fellow countrymen.

Thomas's interest, however, was on other matters. "Did you read about the Panama Canal when you were at the Uelands'?"

"It's a funny thing, Thomas. I didn't see a single newspaper the whole time I was there. Not one."

Thomas shook his head. "An attorney would have to keep up with the latest news. Perhaps he reads at his office."

Thomas was probably right. Maria wondered if living in the country had anything to do with it. Everything was so peaceful and serene out there, and the city was so noisy and crowded—and hot. Perhaps Mr. Ueland read the news but didn't choose to bring it home with him.

At any rate, Thomas went on to explain about the historic opening of the canal on August 15. Thomas was fascinated by the mammoth locks that moved ships through the canal. He had talked to Papa about going to school to study engineering, and Papa simply said, "Thomas, you can do anything you put your mind to. This is America."

After the rock and its threatening message had been thrown through the window, several incidents of vandalism had occurred at the homes of the other union officers. But nothing more had happened at the Schmidt home. Papa continued to attend union meetings. He told the family that the group was growing each time they met.

"Other courageous mill workers are now joining us," he said one evening at supper. "Some from the Pillsbury Mill and some from Washburn. Soon we'll have the large numbers we need to negotiate. There've been rumors that our wages are to be cut soon."

Mama looked at him with worry in her eyes. "Again?"

Maria knew that even with Mama's salary from the freight company, there was barely enough money to make ends meet. It was all the fault of those rich people. They made the workers grovel, while they lived in comfort. The pay cuts were never big—just a penny here and a penny there. But for hard-working men, each and every penny counted for a great deal.

Anger filled Maria's heart. She wished she could do something to stop the injustice. Papa came home so weary from the long hours, especially as the summer days grew hotter and hotter. Some evenings Papa acted as though he could hardly hold his eyes open to read the Bible before prayer time. One evening Mama took the Bible from him.

"Here, Franz," she said gently. "What if I read the selection this evening?"

"And I can do it tomorrow evening," Thomas quickly added.

"We can all take turns," Libby added in her usual bubbly way.

Papa looked around at them and smiled. "A blessed man I am to have such a kind, thoughtful family," he said.

His gentle words made tears burn in Maria's eyes.

CHAPTER 13

Back to School

In spite of the overpowering heat, Curt spent a great deal of time in his darkroom. Papa teased that there was no room to store even a shovel or hammer these days. But they knew Papa was proud of all that Curt was learning.

One afternoon when Aunt Josephine happened to stop by, Curt said, "Aunt Josephine, I caught you in one of my photographs. Want me to show you?"

Libby took charge of Joanne and Lloyd while Aunt Josephine sat down at the kitchen table with Baby Howard in her lap. "What a question," she said to Curt, smiling broadly. "Of course I want to see it. Will I have a copy of my own, or will I have to purchase it from this up-and-coming businessman photographer?"

Curt looked at her for a moment. "Stay right there," he said. "I'll be right back."

"As if I would go any place in this miserable heat."

Maria busied herself by fixing her aunt and cousins glasses of lemonade while Curt hurried up the stairs. He stored his finished photographs between old newspapers beneath the bed.

When he returned, he had several photos in hand. "These are from the fair," he told her. "Look at this one of you." He placed it on the table out of Howard's reach.

Aunt Josephine leaned over to gaze at the photos. "Why, Curt Schmidt! These are splendid photos!"

Maria was surprised at the glowing compliment. Truthfully, she'd not paid too much attention to Curt's new hobby, feeling it was a bit too expensive for their household. But now she leaned over to look as well.

The first photo showed Aunt Josephine standing at the edge of the tent, handing a man a cup of lemonade. The sign WOMEN SHOULD VOTE was emblazoned just above her head. The other women and various visitors to the tent were in the background. There were several other photos of the tent and all the goings-on of the suffrage association at the fair. Just looking at them made Maria remember all the heat and dust and the rude men who made unkind remarks. They were good photos, all right.

"I have others of the midway, but I thought you'd be more interested in these," Curt said in his soft voice.

"I'm not the only one who would be interested in these," Aunt Josephine told him. "Did you not think that Mrs. Ueland and the association might want to purchase copies of these?"

Curt's eyes grew wide. He shook his head. "No, ma'am."

"Can you put these in something?" Aunt Josephine asked. "I'd like to show them to Clara and see what she thinks. They use these kinds of things in the papers and pamphlets that the association distributes."

"I can wrap them in newspaper with pasteboard to keep them flat." Before anyone could say another word, Curt had grabbed them all up and run back upstairs.

When Aunt Josephine left that day, she took Curt's photographs. The next time they went to the Andersons' to visit, Aunt Josephine presented a surprised Curt with a check for five dollars. They all laughed at the shocked expression on the boy's face.

Still chuckling, Uncle Robert said, "Tell me, Curt, what in the world are you going to do with all that money?"

Curt didn't hesitate a minute. "Three dollars will go to Mama and Papa, and the other two will go to purchase more photo supplies."

Curt stared at the five-dollar check in his hand. Maria was so proud of him, she felt she would almost burst.

School was due to begin in a week. Maria had hoped against hope that the money she'd saved over the summer would go to purchase a new dress for Libby. But it just wasn't to be. When it came time for the four Schmidt children to purchase new school shoes, there wasn't enough money to cover the cost. So Maria put her savings into the family till, very pleased that she could help but still sorry she couldn't get Libby a new dress.

Mama unpacked two of Maria's old school dresses from the trunk upstairs. The castoffs would be cut down for Libby's school dresses. Though the dresses were worn and had a few holes from where Maria had played hard with her brothers, Maria and Mama were able to patch the rip and use the best pieces to make two serviceable dresses.

Libby took out the old stitches, and Maria trimmed the pieces and sewed them back together again. They had moved the treadle machine close to the back door, where they would catch any little breeze.

"Maria?" Libby asked. She sat cross-legged on the floor with her doll Florence close by her side.

Maria glanced up from the machine. Her sister's face was screwed up with concern. "What is it, Libby?"

"Do you think you or I will ever have nice dresses? Really nice dresses?"

"Sure we will. Especially you. You're so pretty, you'll snag a rich husband sure as anything."

"But that's a long time off. Do you think it will happen anytime sooner?"

Maria had difficulty understanding her little sister's need for nice things. The two of them were so different. Maria wished she never had to wear a dress at all. She loved wearing her brother's blouses, which were so much more comfortable than her high-collared dresses.

When Maria didn't answer, Libby was quick to add, "I don't mean to complain. I'm thankful we have these things."

"Are you saying you wish I'd taken a little better care of my dresses?" Maria teased.

Libby held up a skirt piece with two fair-sized rips in it. "You could have done a little better by me," she replied, making them both laugh.

"I have a few pennies saved back," Maria said. "We could find some ribbon pieces at the five-and-ten. We can use that to make your dresses more fussy."

"Some of the girls have such fashionable frocks with satin and silk fabrics and all frothy with lace and ruffles," Libby said. "Is it wrong to like things like that?"

Maria felt these were questions Mama should be answering. Suddenly she remembered Mrs. Ueland, so she began to tell the story of how she knew of a little girl with no father and a widowed mama and little brother. She told how they had to live in crowded rooms above a hardware store, but that the girl was the prettiest girl at Washington High School and everyone in school liked her. Well, at least that's how Torvald had described his mama.

"I'm not sure if it's wrong to want pretty dresses," Maria concluded. "But I think it's more important to work on what's inside of us instead of what's on the outside of us."

Maria learned she would have done well to take her own advice. When school began, none of the Schmidts were prepared for the problems that awaited those who happened to have German-sounding last names. The slurs Maria heard on the playground and whispered in the classroom hit her as hard as those German guns she'd read about in the paper.

Charles Briggs was the one with the most to say, as usual. "Dirty Hun," he whispered under his breath when he walked by her desk. "Baby killer." At recess, he and other boys made up several chants about the ruthless, mindless Germans. "Kraut-eaters," they said.

But it wasn't only what Maria heard that bothered her. It was how she felt. Something strange was in the air. The other kids looked at her funny and walked around her—as though a sign were hung about her neck that said DANGER, STAY AWAY. Last year Evelyn and Cathy had twittered about her and gaped at her. Now they acted as though she didn't exist.

Torvald was the pleasant exception to it all. Though he was quiet as ever in class, he smiled at her. Maria wasn't sure if he understood the extent to which she was being avoided, but he seemed to know. Even the eighth-grade teacher, Mr. Denning, was aloof and distant when dealing with German-American students. He'd certainly not behaved that way with last year's class. But last year, Germany had not attacked and ransacked Belgium.

Based on the latest news reports, Germany was on a straight course for Paris. Soon all of France would be overrun and destroyed by Germany. Maria had no control over any of that. Nor did she agree with it. But what could she say? No one was asking her.

The very first day of school, as they walked home, Curt was extremely quiet, and Libby fought back tears. Maria knew their treatment had been as bad or worse than hers. Each seemed to know what the other was thinking, but the pain was too deep to talk about. Maria made stabs at light conversation, but it was of little use.

Thomas might have helped with his usual positive outlook, but he now had an after-school job in an office downtown. He served as an errand boy for the German engineering firm of Wahrmund and Strackbein. He wouldn't be home until Mama arrived, and Maria missed him.

"Be sure and change your clothes," she said to Curt and Libby when they arrived home. A silly thing to say. No one needed to tell them to change.

Together Maria and Libby worked in the kitchen to prepare supper, while Curt went out to his darkroom. As Maria whipped up a batch of *spätzle* noodles, she wondered how she might quit school and go to work. That seemed to be the only answer. How could she face week after week of such dreadful treatment?

Then she looked over at Libby, who was peeling potatoes at the sink. No. It would be unfair to leave her younger sister to face such treatment alone. She'd have to stick it out, no matter how bad it became. Maybe the war would be over quickly and everyone would just forget about it.

When Mama and Papa asked about their school day that evening, each child quietly said it had been fine. Just fine.

CHAPTER 14

The Children's Canteen

Maria thought it was nothing short of a miracle that Mama allowed her to continue the paper route after school began. Perhaps Mama simply couldn't think of any good reason to make her stop. Especially now that she was doing such a good job. Not even Mama could argue that their family couldn't use the extra money. It took a lot of groceries to feed four children, especially since Thomas never seemed to get full.

Through that first week of September, the younger newsboys kept mentioning something about a Miss Elsa. It seemed this person—this Miss Elsa—had opened a place where they could go to eat breakfast each morning. Maria was fascinated. Who would do such a thing?

"*We* ain't goin' over there," Liver Lid told the Schmidts, jabbing a thumb at himself and then at Tony. "What I means to say is, we two don't need no fancy dame dishing no free handouts to us."

"Yeah," Tony added, "but them little ones, they needs it. We been seein' to it they get over there each morning."

"You mean someone's just come in and set up a kitchen?" Thomas asked. That was exactly what Maria wanted to ask them, but only Thomas could do it without causing offense.

"It ain't down in the Flats," Tony said. "It's in an old abandoned storefront on Second Street."

Liver Lid pulled off his cap, scratched his rumpled hair, and put the cap back on. The cap was a ratty old thing that had seen better days. "Don't know what to make of it," he said. "Probably just some goofy do-gooder. Get a little scare into her, and she'll be gone."

"Too good to last, that's what I say," Tony added.

They were interrupted by the men who brought the newspaper bundles out on the dock. But as Maria threw her papers that morning, she couldn't stop thinking about a lady named Miss Elsa. Someone else in this city cared about these boys, and Maria wanted to meet that someone. But how? Mama would never allow her to go that close to Bohemian Flats. It was simply too dangerous.

All that day, this new thought kept Maria's attention away from the bad feelings at school. She'd never really been close friends with the few other German kids in her class. But now she began to feel a real kinship toward them.

Headlines on Saturday, September 12, made Maria feel almost jubilant. The French had stopped the Germans from hitting Paris. Strange as it seemed, the Germans had actually retreated more than eighty miles.

"This probably means it's all over," Curt said with a note of hope in his voice. "Sometimes I find myself wishing. . ." He stopped and glanced around the alleyway. But the three of them were the only ones in the alley folding papers.

"Wishing what?" Maria asked, though she could almost read his mind.

"That the Germans would get soundly trounced."

"I know, Curt," Thomas said. "I feel the same way."

"You do?"

"Me, too." Maria picked up her bag and slung it over her shoulder. "That makes it unanimous, so I'm sure it's bound to happen. And," she added as she adjusted the weight of the heavy papers, "I'm not the least bit ashamed of it."

When the route was finished that morning, Maria finally got up the courage to ask Thomas to take her to meet Miss Elsa. Since it was

Saturday, the day was free.

Thomas looked at her. "You know what Mama would say if she ever found out you were that close to the river."

"There's nothing wrong with the river. Papa works right on the river."

"Maria, you know what I mean."

She nodded. "I know, Thomas, but I've wanted to help those little guys who don't have anyone or anything. Now I find there's someone who thinks the way I do about them, and I can't even find out who she is. It's just not fair."

Thomas finally gave in. "All right. I'll take you there after we eat breakfast, but we'll only stay a few minutes. Just long enough so you can see this Miss Elsa, then we're coming right back home."

"Are we telling Mama?" Curt wanted to know.

"Only if she asks," Maria said.

So Curt and Libby stayed at the house while Thomas walked with Maria down to Second Street. It wasn't a very nice part of Minneapolis. They had no trouble finding the old storefront. A makeshift sign outside said CHILDREN'S CANTEEN.

"What a perfectly wonderful idea," Maria said when she saw it.

A person couldn't see too much through the dust film on the plate glass windows. Thomas opened the door for Maria, and she stepped inside. It was pretty empty. A few plank tables were scattered about. Two or three cracker barrels and several wooden crates of fruit sat over against one wall. A young lady sat writing in a ledger at one of the tables. A very pretty young lady she was. She looked up as they came in.

"Well," she said, "you don't look like the usual fare that comes tromping up from the Flats. How may I help you?"

She stood, and Maria could see she was a slim little thing with a waist no bigger than a hand span. Her dress, a pale blue summer linen, had a square-cut neckline and sleeves that went only to her elbows. It gave the appearance of elegance, yet was so very cool in the September heat. Fitted into the woman's pompadour was a strand of silk rosettes the color of her dress. Her cheeks were rosy, as though she spent a good deal of time outdoors.

"Excuse me," Thomas said, because Maria had lost her voice. "We're looking for Miss Elsa. Could you tell us where to find her?"

The young lady smiled, and her clear blue eyes lit up. "Look no farther."

Maria hoped her mouth wasn't gaping. She'd pictured some motherly type lady would be in charge of such an undertaking. "You're Miss Elsa?"

"I am. Is there something wrong?"

Maria was at a loss for words. Thomas stepped up and held out his hand. "I'm Thomas Schmidt, and this is my sister Maria. We throw papers for the *Tribune* and know many of the newsboys. They've been talking about this place, and my sister here. . . Well, my sister is interested in helping the boys. She wanted to see. . ."

"See what kind of daft person would come to such a place?" Miss Elsa laughed. "Now you see."

"Please," Maria said, "I didn't mean. . ."

"I'm teasing of course." Miss Elsa turned to Maria and shook her hand as well. "I know you didn't mean such a thing. But some people do, you know. Most of the businessmen I talk to think I'm out of my mind."

"Businessmen?"

Miss Elsa nodded. "Businessmen. I approach them to become sponsors—people to give money or clothing or food or whatever. A few of them listen to me, but most dismiss me as just plain daft."

Her face didn't look as though this fact bothered her at all. She seemed more amused by it than anything else.

"Why don't you just set up an orphanage?" Thomas asked in his practical manner. "Or join forces with the existing orphanages?"

Miss Elsa looked Thomas right in the eyes. "That's a very good question, young man. This work is quite different from an orphanage. It may be that we'll funnel some of these street children into an orphanage, but their daily needs are my concern—food and clothing and," she added, "their souls."

Maria noted a leather-bound Bible lying on the table. "Whatever gave you such an idea?" she asked.

"I've just spent two years doing this type of work in the slums of New York City."

Thomas's eyebrows went up. Maria could tell he was impressed.

"The work there is up and running now, with dozens of volunteers and many supporters. I'm the adventurer. I relish a challenge. Starting the work is what I enjoy doing. My parents had been begging me to come back to Minneapolis, so I decided to create the same type of work here."

Miss Elsa waved a delicate hand at the room. "It's not much now," she said, "but just wait. By the time the snow flies, I hope to have it quite cozy in here."

Maria was fascinated by this lovely girl. An adventurer she called herself, and yet she was every inch an elegant lady.

They heard a motorcar pull up out front. "There's Mama and my brother now," Miss Elsa said.

Maria turned as the creaking door opened. In walked Torvald Ueland.

She turned back to Miss Elsa. "This is your brother?"

She nodded. "It is. Torvald," she said, "come here. There's someone I'd like you to meet."

Torvald smiled. "We've met, thank you, Elsa."

Then Mrs. Ueland walked in wearing her impressive hat with the ostrich plumes. "Well, well, as I live and breathe. If it isn't our Maria.

How are you, my dear?" She glanced at Elsa and said, "I certainly hope you've recruited this young girl. She's capable of handling the work of about three her size."

Elsa was laughing. "My, what a small world. You all know one another."

Mrs. Ueland quickly explained to Elsa how Maria had helped at the fair, then at the fund-raiser.

Thomas, however, hadn't met any of them. As they were introduced, he said, "I do know your son Rolf from school, but not well."

Elsa turned to Maria. "You said you have compassion for the street children. Does that mean you'd care to volunteer here?"

"Oh, I would." Maria glanced over at Thomas. "But I'm not sure Mama would. . ."

"What if I telephoned your mama and talked with her?" Mrs. Ueland put in. "I can explain to her about Elsa's previous work and assure her you'll be perfectly safe here."

"Would you do that?" Maria's heart was beginning to race.

"Of course I would. Now Elsa's about to lock up, I believe. May we drive you to your home?"

"No need for that. We can walk," Thomas said politely.

Maria knew he wanted to ride in their touring car just as much as she did. It was much classier than Uncle Robert's Model T.

"But if you insist," Maria added quickly.

Elsa put her arm affectionately about Maria's shoulder. "We insist."

———

Mrs. Ueland telephoned the Brauns that very evening, asking for Mama. They talked quite a long while. Maria had told Mama beforehand all that had transpired and for her to expect the call. Mama was upset that Maria had gone into that part of town. "But," she quickly added, "I suppose with Thomas there, you were safe."

"I should say she was," Thomas put in, giving Mama his lop-sided grin.

After the conversation with Mrs. Ueland, Mama and Papa agreed to allow Maria to donate a few hours a week at the canteen. Suddenly there was a bright spot in Maria's life.

That night as she lay in the small bed with Libby snuggled next to her, Maria thought a great deal about Elsa. Rolf and Torvald had told her how their three older sisters played ball with the boys, rode horses, and swam in the lake. But Elsa didn't seem at all like a tomboy. Could a woman be assertive, adventurous, and all she wanted to be—and still be a lady?

CHAPTER 15
New Clothes

The hours Maria spent with Elsa were wonderful. Together they scrubbed down the walls and windows and swept and scrubbed the hardwood floors. As they worked, Maria learned much about Elsa and her ideas. She and her sisters had all graduated from college. Not girls' school, but college.

"Mama taught us early that the boys could do some of the household chores and we girls could work out in the barn. We all took part in everything that needed to be done—without distinction. So when it came time to go to college, we never thought twice about attending."

Maria remembered how Torvald never minded working in the kitchen. What an interesting family this was.

For her part, Maria told Elsa all she knew about the boys who hawked papers on the street corners for a few pennies each day. How the boys from the *Tribune* and those from the *Journal* were enemies. Several of the boys also had shoeshine boxes and worked at that after the papers were sold. She explained that the older boys were too proud to be seen inside the canteen.

Elsa listened and voiced her appreciation for all the information. "It's much the same way in New York, although I found the boys there to be much tougher and mean-spirited than the ones here. It won't take long to win their trust and confidence," she said. "We'll rely on God's love."

By mid-September, the heat broke at long last, and a cool north breeze swept the heaviness and lethargy from the city. Sleeping through the cool nights was a relief.

Elsa planned to have the canteen stocked with clothes and food before the bitter cold of winter arrived. That meant there was much work to be done.

One day as Elsa and Maria sat at one of the tables working on lists of merchants to visit, Elsa looked at Maria and said, "You're such a pretty girl, Maria. Have you ever thought of wearing your hair up?"

Maria felt her face growing warm. So many of the girls in eighth grade wore their hair up, but she didn't feel it was worth the fuss and bother. "I've tried, but it won't stay," she said lamely.

Elsa nodded as she reached out to take one of Maria's braids in her hand. "Mm. Silky, as I thought. It does take a little practice. Surely your mama has a curling iron."

"She does. It's just too much trouble."

"Here. . ." Elsa started unfastening the braids before Maria could protest. "I can show you quick as a wink. Come into the back."

There was no sense arguing. Before Maria knew it, both her braids were unfastened, and Elsa had pulled a hairbrush from her bag, along with a container of hairpins and a nice hair comb. She handed a small tortoiseshell mirror to Maria and said, "There are tricks to this, you know." She chuckled as she heated a curling iron over a hot plate. "And whether we like it or not, we really do need to learn them."

Point by point, she not only demonstrated the method, but then she took it all down and made Maria do it herself. Twice! With curl in her hair, it did go up easier and stay up better.

Elsa nodded her approval. "Nice," she said. "Very nice. Now I've been thinking. In our attic there are trunks full of dresses my sisters and I used to wear. With three of us, we had plenty. I was shorter than you when I was your age, but Anne, she was the tall, slender one."

Maria immediately thought of Libby. "It's my little sister Libby who longs for pretty dresses," she said.

"Are you telling me you don't?"

Maria shook her head. "Not really. It's not as important to me."

"But every girl needs a pretty dress," Elsa insisted. "Besides, if you're going to accompany me as we solicit help from these business-men, a nice dress or two might come in handy."

Maria was quiet, trying not to appear as shocked as she was feel-ing. "You want *me* to go with you?"

"I certainly do."

"Then I'd be pleased to wear one of your nice dresses."

"Remember! After I give them to you, they'll be *your* nice dresses!"

That evening the family fussed over Maria's new hairdo. Libby just stared. "Why, Maria, you look almost like a grown-up with your hair like that."

The comment made Maria look one more time in the mirror that hung above the sink. Did it change her looks that much?

Maria knew she couldn't formally accept the dresses until it was cleared with Mama. She waited until she and Mama were alone, be-cause she didn't want Libby to hear unless it was a sure thing. Since Mama now knew Mrs. Ueland better, she was agreeable. However, Maria felt a twinge of guilt when Mama softly added, "Perhaps one day Papa and I will have what's needed to purchase such things."

"Mama. . ."

"But, no matter," Mama said, brightening quickly. "It'll be a joy to see the two of you in nicer dresses."

Maria knew it hurt Mama that there were many things they could not afford. But Papa always said, "We are fed, clothed, and sheltered. That is sufficient."

"What's a 'stalemate'?" Tony asked as he lugged his bundle down from the dock.

Throughout September, the headlines had not been as big and blaring as they had been a few weeks earlier.

"A stalemate," Thomas explained, "means neither side is going anywhere. No one is winning."

Neither Tony nor Liver Lid could read well, but they knew enough to make out the headlines. Sometimes Thomas would read them out loud if he thought there were words the boys might not know. Thomas was always careful not to insult the boys.

"They're digging trenches and sitting still," Curt said, looking up from the paper he was reading. He shook his head in bewilderment. "Dumbest thing I ever heard of. How can anyone win the war if they just sit there lobbing shells at one another?"

Maria didn't care how deep they dug their trenches, just so the whole mess had a chance to calm down a bit.

The next Saturday when Maria arrived to help out at the canteen, Elsa had brought the dresses as promised. It became a very special day for Maria. Elsa was so excited, she urged Maria to go to the back and try one on immediately. Maria was puzzled as to why Elsa should be so excited about giving away her old clothes. But she had to admit the excitement was contagious.

"I tried to pick out ones I thought your mama would approve of," Elsa said, smiling. "I want these gifts to be blessings, not troublemakers."

Maria knew she was referring to high necklines and long sleeves. Elsa put a dress into Maria's hands and gave her a little push toward the back room. "After you put that on, I'll let you see the ones I picked out for Libby."

Maria went into the back room where they kept their personal belongings. When she unfolded the dress, out fell a pair of lacy bloomers and a fine silk chemise. It was almost more than Maria could bear. She bit her lip to hold back tears.

She slipped into the nice things, then pulled the dress over her head. It fit perfectly. The fabric was tightly woven and sturdy, not thin like her cotton print. Maria studied the tucks and seams and wondered if Lizzie Higgins might have sewn this dress years ago when Elsa was still in grammar school.

Elsa had fastened a mirror on the wall above a large sink. Maria stepped over to take a look. She couldn't stop staring. The powder blue fabric looked quite fetching against her fair skin and corn-silk hair. Was she truly seeing her own reflection? Who was this girl looking back at her? This total stranger?

"You're certainly taking your time," Elsa called out. "I'm out here consumed with curiosity."

Maria opened the door and stepped out. Elsa let out a very un-ladylike whistle. "I knew when I first saw you that there was a pretty lady hiding inside. And here she is!"

That day Maria walked alongside Elsa as they visited a number of businessmen to explain the goals of the Children's Canteen. Some agreed to help, others did not. All were kind, and no one refused to listen.

"My mama always told us girls, 'When you look like a lady and act like a lady, you'll be treated like a lady,' " Elsa told Maria. Then she added, "But that doesn't mean we're less than men when it comes to abilities and brains."

Maria listened and learned. Then she thought of what Mama had said to her about the potter and the clay. Perhaps the potter had been right after all. When she was dressed in such a nice frock, she felt almost pleased to be a girl.

Libby couldn't stop oohing and ahhing over the three new dresses Maria brought home to her. Actually, there was a fourth dress in the bundle, but Mama and Maria agreed to hide it from Libby and use it as a Christmas gift. The navy twill trimmed in cranberry velvet would make a perfect Christmas dress.

"All I ever prayed for was one new dress," Libby kept saying, "and here I have three. God truly does give more than we ask for." After giving Mama and Maria both a giant bear hug, she said, "Now at school when they call me a Hun, at least I'll be a well-dressed Hun."

And that was the first time any of them had said out loud what was happening to them at school. Mama didn't act shocked at all. That made Maria wonder if Mama had heard some of the same cruel remarks at her workplace.

As autumn progressed, the awful teasing lightened up in Maria's classroom. Or it could have been the fact that working with Elsa made Maria care a little less what the other students said and did. Not even Evelyn or Cathy mattered much to her now. Wearing the dresses Elsa had given her, with her hair piled high, Maria had gained a new measure of confidence.

"You're God's child. Always walk with dignity, and hold your head high," Elsa would whisper to her before they entered into a place of business to solicit donations of money or goods.

Maria began whispering the same words to herself each day when she arrived at school, and then she began saying it to Curt and Libby, as well. It drew them closer together and made the worst days easier to bear.

CHAPTER 16

Pay Cuts

"Are we going to set out our shoes for St. Nicholas this year?" Libby asked one day in early December.

The Advent wreath, covered with greenery and holly berries, sat in the center of the kitchen table. The first candle had been lit the previous Sunday, the first Sunday after Thanksgiving. Many people in the city celebrated Advent and lit candles each Sunday before Christmas—not just German families. However, only German children set out their shoes by the fireplace on December 5—St. Nicholas Eve—so that St. Nicholas could slip in at night and fill the shoes with candy and fruit.

Ever since the war began, the Schmidts had grown wary of doing German things and saying German words. Maria thought it was kind of eerie. So much had changed in so short a time.

Earlier in November, Maria and Thomas had both celebrated their birthdays, which were two days apart. Maria's came on the tenth and Thomas's on the twelfth. Papa joked that he was thankful he didn't have to go to two more flickers—especially just two days apart. But neither Maria nor Thomas cared a great deal about the flickers. And Maria wouldn't have cared if she never saw another newsreel like the one they'd seen back in August.

After turning thirteen, Maria expected she would feel much older, but it didn't happen. Putting her hair up and wearing the dresses Elsa had given her made her feel older than celebrating a birthday. Now the month of November was past and Christmas was just around the corner.

Papa mulled over Libby's question about St. Nicholas Eve. At last he answered, "I don't see what it would harm to put out the shoes as we always have done."

"Well, Mrs. Braun said we shouldn't," Libby reported.

"Since when did you ever do what Mrs. Braun says?" Thomas asked.

Mrs. Braun did boss them around quite a bit. Recently the Schmidts had been concerned for their neighbors since vandals had thrown a bucket of black paint on the plate glass windows of Mr. Braun's leather goods shop and painted unkind words on the brick walls.

Maria remembered when Mr. Braun had scolded Papa about causing trouble in the neighborhood because of being active in the labor union. Now it was Mr. Braun who was being targeted, and there wasn't much anyone could do about it. A person might quit being a member of the labor union, but how did one stop being a German?

So in spite of everything, the children set their shoes by the small fireplace in the parlor. Of course, not even Libby truly believed anymore that St. Nicholas came in the night, but the tradition added a festive air to the holiday season.

Now that Advent had arrived, Maria, Libby, and Mama began baking the *stollen*, a sweet bread that was coated in snowy powdered sugar. And soon they would bake the *lebkuchen*—spicy ginger cookies.

Mama always said, "No one can celebrate Christmas like the Germans. They begin with St. Nicholas Day and don't finish until Epiphany."

She was right. But this year it was different. The German community had cut back drastically on their scheduled festivities.

Winter came with a vengeance, bringing early snows and freezing temperatures. But many of the newsboys—thanks to Elsa and her hard work—wore new mittens, stockings without holes, and knitted stocking caps pulled down over their ears. And the children who stopped by the canteen in the mornings were given bowls of hot oatmeal. Tony and Liver Lid and the older boys did odd jobs for Elsa in exchange for their food and clothes.

Maria wished she could help Elsa with the cooking every morning, but of course she couldn't. She had her own family's breakfast to prepare and her paper route to throw.

Two weeks before Christmas, Maria was helping Elsa hang garlands and brightly colored paper chains around the canteen. More tables and chairs filled the room now, and the storefront was clean and inviting. Off to one side Elsa had a flannel board where she told the children Bible stories. A heating stove stood in one corner, and a merchant had agreed to donate coal to heat the place.

Elsa planned to have a party for the children just before Christmas. "It won't be much this year," she'd explained to Maria. "But just wait 'til next year when we have a full staff." Elsa stepped up on a stepladder with a hammer in hand, and Maria handed her the decorations and nails. As they worked, the subject turned to different causes that were important to people.

"That's how my papa feels about the labor union," Maria said. "Even though we've received nasty threats, he won't quit."

"That does take courage," Elsa agreed as she hammered another nail into place. On the nail, she hooked another loop of the paper chain.

"Until unions gain the respect from all citizens and from government officials," Maria continued, "the insensitive, greedy, wealthy people will continue to wield control over the..." Then she stopped. "Oh, I didn't mean...."

"You're partly right, my dear. But only partly. There're some wealthy people who do oppress those beneath them—but not all of them do."

"I didn't mean *your* family is like that."

Elsa laughed. "Why, Maria, my dear, I take that as a compliment, but one could hardly call our family wealthy. What with so many mouths

Mama and Papa had to feed, so many of us to send off to college, and a big mortgage to pay off, it was nip and tuck many times at our house." She reached out her hand. "Another nail, please." The hammer banged again.

"You must remember, Maria, that wealth is relative. Did it ever occur to you that to the children living down in the Flats, *you* are the wealthy one?"

Maria thought about that idea.

"Another nail and more paper chain, please."

As they finished decorating and left for the evening, Maria couldn't stop thinking about Elsa's words. To someone like Tony, Maria lived in a palace, ate like a queen, and dressed like royalty. It was an intriguing thought.

Christmas came on Friday that year. The Monday morning prior to the holiday, one of the men on the dock at the news office called for the boys to gather around because he had an announcement to make.

Maria usually paid scant attention to those men. They were never kind to the boys, treating them as though they were no better than the rats that skittered through the alleyways. But when he said "announcement," she moved in a little closer and listened.

The man told the boys that they would be required to sell more papers each day, and their pay per paper was to be cut by two cents each. A loud groan went up from the boys, and Tony and Liver Lid and the older ones made shouts of protest.

"Aw, shut your traps," the man yelled back at them over the noise. "You oughta be glad we even let you handle our papers."

"Thomas," Maria said, nudging her brother. "They can't do that, can they? It's so unfair."

But Thomas's mind was on another matter. "Hey!" he called out.

"What about those of us who have paid subscription routes?"

Maria knew that route customers paid a few cents more for having their papers delivered.

"Them with routes gets a three-cent cut," the man yelled back. "Times is tough, you know. We all gotta make sacrifices."

Thomas's face went sort of empty. Thomas, who usually had a witty answer for everything, had no lopsided grin now. "Times aren't *that* tough," he said. He didn't say it very loud, but the man heard.

"Hey!" he hollered down. "Ain't your name Schmidt?"

Thomas stood up to his full height. "You know it is."

"Well, you Kraut-eaters oughta be the last ones to complain. Be lucky we let your kind stay on at all." With that, he turned around and stomped back into the building.

Your kind. Maria stood frozen. They'd all heard the awful words. When hate-filled words came to the Schmidt children individually, and if they never discussed it, they could pretend it never happened. This was different. She and Curt and Thomas had all heard the cutting words, and from an adult.

"Aw, they're a bunch of creeps," Liver Lid said, waving his hand toward the dock. "That's all they are. We'll come up here in the middle of the night and make a mess outta this place. And we got enough boys to do it, too."

Thomas shook his head. "Don't do anything foolish, Liver Lid," he told them. "It's just not worth the grief it'd bring." He picked up his bundle. "Like he said," Thomas said in a softer voice, "let's be thankful we have the jobs at all."

CHAPTER 17

The Riot

As Maria, Curt, and Libby walked home from school through the snow and bone-chilling cold, Maria couldn't stop thinking about the pay cut. It made her so furious she could hardly think about school. How dare they be so cruel? And right before Christmas!

Suddenly a voice called from behind them. "Schmidts! Curt! Maria! Stop a minute!"

Maria whirled about in her tracks. It was Kicker Joe. He was panting and could hardly catch his breath. "Tony sent me. 'Get Thomas,' he says to me. 'Get Thomas Schmidt.' "

"What is it?" Maria asked. "Is Tony hurt?"

Kicker Joe held his side and sucked in his breath. "I ran fast as I could. I gotta get Thomas."

"Thomas is not here," Maria said. "He has an after-school job."

Kicker Joe's face fell and tears welled up in his eyes. "Oh, no. What am I gonna do?"

"We can get him," Curt said.

The boy looked up at Curt with hopeful eyes. "Fast?"

"What's the matter, Kicker Joe? Tell us what's happened," Maria said.

Libby stared wide-eyed at this waif dressed in ragged clothing.

"All the boys down at the Flats," Kicker Joe said, "ones from the *Journal* and the *Tribune* both. . .gathering together. Gonna attack the *Tribune* office, they says, and do lots of damage."

"No!" Maria cried. "They can't do that. They'll never have any jobs then." Maria turned to Libby. "Libby, you go straight home and stay there. Curt, you go to Wahrmund and Strackbein's. Get Thomas as fast as you can. Bring him down to the Flats."

"Maria." Curt's eyes were big. "What're you gonna do?"

"They trust me, Curt. I'm going with Kicker Joe and try to talk to them."

"No, Maria," Curt protested. "You don't know those boys from the *Journal*. They're real tough guys. Mama'll kill me for letting you go."

"We're wasting time, Curt. Go—and hurry. Libby? Straight home, you hear me?"

"Yes, Maria." Libby took out for home on a dead run.

Maria turned to follow Kicker Joe, terrified, but knowing someone had to stop those crazy boys. What insanity this was. They'd only make things a hundred times worse.

By the time she and Kicker Joe reached the brow of the hill over-looking the Flats, Maria's side ached and her lungs were on fire from the icy cold. Early winter dusk was settling over the city.

"Down this way." Kicker Joe motioned to her.

A set of rickety wooden steps seemed to go down and down end-lessly. Spread out on the lower banks by the river was the infamous Flats. It was nothing but crowded squalor for several miles, and it looked more pitiful than anything she could have imagined. Every type and sort of makeshift shelter was set up on that narrow strip of land. Tiny wisps of gray smoke curled up from many of them. Everything inside her wanted to run back home. What was she thinking of?

"Come on. Hurry!" Kicker Joe said as he scrambled down the steps.

Maria clung to the splintery banister because the packed snow on the wooden steps made them treacherously slick. Halfway down, she stopped to catch her breath. But only for a minute, because Kicker Joe hadn't even looked back to see if she was following.

As they approached the Flats, Maria could hear a rumbling noise. Then she realized it was the voices of a mob of angry boys. At first she could only hear them, but as they rounded a bend, she saw them. They were armed with clubs. Some had knives out. Several carried torches.

"Kicker Joe," she said, "how will I find Tony and Liver Lid?"

"I'll show ya."

But as he slipped around the noisy crowd, a boy turned and saw Maria. "There's some of that fancy rich trash," he called out, pointing to her. "They're the ones who starve us out."

Someone shoved her, knocking her to the ground. She felt the wind rush out of her. She tried to call for Tony, but she had no voice.

"Whatta you doin' down in the Flats?" another boy shouted. "Come to laugh? To make sport?"

One of the boys picked her up, then flung her around. Another boy gave her a shove. She stumbled and nearly fell again. "Stop," she cried, gasping for air. "Don't go to the *Tribune*. Please!" she begged.

"Yeah, sure, a lot you care about what we do." She was shoved again.

Just then, Kicker Joe appeared again. Running up to one of the boys, he kicked him hard in the shins. "Leave her be, you dumb *Journal*-carrying lummox!"

"Why, you little shrimp. Look who you're calling a lummox."

Maria was pushed to the ground as they tried to grab Kicker Joe. But he was too fast for them. Dancing out of their reach, he yelled for Tony. Suddenly Tony was there.

"Maria Schmidt!" he called out when he saw her. "You're crazy to come down here." Tony started pushing and shoving guys out of the way. "Stand back. This here's a real lady."

Reluctantly, they stepped back. "If she was a real lady, she'd never have come down here," one boy shouted.

Tony reached down to help her up. "Where's Thomas?" he asked.

"Coming." She gasped for air. Her knit hat had been flung to who knew where, her hair was streaming in her face, and her gloves were torn. Her dress, too, probably.

"You can't do this," she said, looking around at the thin, pitiful faces of the boys. "Please. There's a better way." She stopped again to catch her breath. "Demonstrate. Don't destroy. If you go up there to that office with your clubs and torches, you'll be acting just like the urchins they believe you to be. But I know some of you. You're better than that."

"We ain't better," cried one of the boys who had pushed her. "And that's that! They make the rules!"

Tony turned to him and said, "We can be better if we wanna be."

"He's right," Maria said, louder now so they could all hear. "My papa's had his wages cut at the flour mill, but those men wouldn't destroy the place. Instead, they organize. If you'd stop fighting one another and join forces, you could make a difference."

"Don't nobody listen to a dame," came a voice from the crowd.

"You've listened to *this* dame, Freddie," came a woman's voice from the stairs. "You listen to me every morning when I dish up your hot oatmeal!"

It was Elsa! And Thomas and Curt were with her. Maria almost cried with relief and joy.

The crowd broke apart to let them through. Thomas ran to Maria and held her tight. "Thank God, you're safe," he whispered.

Elsa pointed to Maria and said, "This is a wise woman who's talking to you. She's speaking truth. Now let's find out who wants to fight and destroy and who prefers to demonstrate and remain orderly. Let's see you take a real stand."

Tony stepped forward. "I'll demonstrate."

Liver Lid and Kicker Joe were by his side. "Count us in!"

"Aw, you sissies," someone hollered out. But more and more boys stepped forward to stand with the ones who wanted a peaceful solution to the problem. When it was done, there were many more who stepped forward than those who did not. Those who were left quickly dispersed.

Elsa started to speak again, but Tony said, "Wait a minute, Miss Elsa. Go up on the steps where we can see and hear you."

Maria watched as Thomas took Miss Elsa's arm and helped her ascend the slippery steps. She turned to speak to the boys. "Now that I know you truly want to abide by the law and want to make a difference, I have a team to join forces with your group. How many of you are willing to meet me in front of the *Tribune* office at the crack of dawn tomorrow and carry signs and picket?"

Every hand went up.

"Good," she said. "Now go home and get some sleep. You'll meet your team members first thing in the morning. Together, we'll show the owners of the *Tribune* that we won't stand for this treatment of our newsboys."

As Elsa drove Maria, Thomas, and Curt to their house, Thomas asked her, "What's your plan for tomorrow. Who's your team?"

Elsa smiled. "All of Mama's hundreds of club members across the city."

Maria felt her heart fall to her stomach. Elsa was counting on those women to help the poor ragged boys from down in Bohemian Flats? That would never work!

When they got home, Mama was upset and frightened. She was even more shocked to see Maria's disheveled appearance. But Elsa came inside to explain everything.

"Your daughter is quite a hero," she said to Mama. "She kept the boys diverted until we arrived. Otherwise, who knows what they might have done?"

Mama helped Maria out of her coat and began to tend to her cuts and scratches.

"Mrs. Schmidt," Elsa said, "I'd like your permission to pick up your children in the morning and take them with me for this demonstration. They may miss a few hours of school, but I promise to take good care of them. And I'll deliver them to their schools just as soon as I can."

Mama's face was a mixture of pride and concern. "And I've been worried about Franz becoming involved in a strike," she said. "Instead it's my children." But in the end she gave permission.

The next morning, the sidewalks in front of the *Tribune* were packed with well-dressed ladies marching up and down, carrying placards that read GUESS WHAT THE NEWSBOYS RECEIVED FOR CHRISTMAS? and DOES SCROOGE LIVE AT THE *TRIBUNE*?

It wasn't light yet, and Maria couldn't believe that these wealthy women came all the way downtown in the freezing weather to take part in such an event. But there they were. Elsa Ueland and her mother were two incredible organizers! They must have been telephoning the entire night long.

Tony stood gazing at them with his arms folded across his stocky chest. "So this is our team? I ain't never seen anything like this in all my born days. That Elsa's a mighty fine lady."

"I'd never have believed it if I hadn't seen it with my own eyes," Thomas said.

"It may not change anything," Maria said, feeling tears well up in her eyes, "but we sure know they care."

And Curt, even though he had no idea what might happen, came armed with his camera.

No copies of the *Tribune* were thrown that morning, nor were any hawked on the street corners. Orphan boys joined with genteel ladies to pace the sidewalk and wait to see what would happen.

CHAPTER 18

Negotiations

After an hour or so of the demonstrators' marching, the executives of the *Tribune* began to arrive. Their faces registered first shock, then anger as they got out of their automobiles. "Don't you women have anything better to do?" one shouted. "Go home, all of you!"

"If you don't leave, I'm calling the police," yelled another. "They'll drag you out of here and lock up the whole lot of you."

Thomas leaned over and whispered to Maria that the man who mentioned the police was the owner of the newspaper, Mr. Dalhart.

Mrs. Ueland and Elsa stepped up to the door, preventing the men from entering. "I'd like a word with you regarding the pay cuts imposed upon these newsboys," Mrs. Ueland said.

"I have nothing to say to you," Mr. Dalhart stated emphatically. "What does a dame know about running a business?"

Elsa spoke up then. "Not only should you rethink this pay cut, but you should be joining with other businessmen to donate funds to the Children's Canteen, where these children are fed each morning and given warm clothing."

"I've never heard of such a place," Mr. Dalhart said.

"I can tell you about it." It was Tony, stepping forward as brave as anything. "First hot breakfast I can remember eating since my mother died five years ago."

"I can tell you about it." Liver Lid was standing by his side. "See these gloves? These were given to me at the canteen. I can't never remember having warm gloves before."

Soon all the boys were shouting and waving their new caps and gloves.

Mrs. Ueland raised her hand for quiet. Turning to Mr. Dalhart once again, she said, "I'm sure the *Journal* would be more than happy to interview us to get the full story about the canteen and how poorly you've treated these boys right before Christmas."

"Don't give me that," Mr. Dalhart said. "The *Journal* pays same as we do."

"No, they don't!" This was Thomas speaking out. "There've been no pay cuts at the *Journal*."

Maria wanted to shush him, but it was too late.

One of the well-dressed women called out, "If you aren't willing to listen to the plight of these children, my household will cancel our *Tribune* subscription and begin taking the *Journal*."

"That goes for me," shouted another.

"And me."

"Count me in." The chants of agreement were deafening.

Mr. Dalhart waved his hands and shouted, "Now, now, ladies. Let's not get carried away. Perhaps we should talk this over."

"Very well," Mrs. Ueland said, "let's talk." Turning to Elsa, she said, "Elsa, you come, and Maria Schmidt and her brother." Then she pointed at Tony. "And you. What's your name?"

"Anthony, ma'am. You can call me Tony."

"Yes, Tony, you come, and bring your pal there." She was now pointing at Liver Lid. She herded them all past the stammering Mr. Dalhart, who still didn't quite know what had hit him.

Maria said to Libby, "You go over and stand by Curt. We'll be back in a few minutes." Libby nodded and did as she was told.

It was a delicious moment for all of them to sit in the plush, top-floor offices of the *Tribune* and have their opinions heard. Now more than ever, Maria understood why Papa sacrificed as he did to remain a part of their workers' union. There was power in unity.

When they emerged, the pay cuts had been rescinded, and the *Tribune* planned to donate a sizable amount of money to the canteen.

Back out on the sidewalk, Maria and Thomas went around to many of the ladies, shaking their gloved hands and thanking them for their help. Several had already been recruited by Elsa to help out in the canteen.

Later they learned that Mrs. Ueland and Elsa had offered to purchase Curt's photos. "The newspaper may never print them," Elsa said, "but we'll post them on the walls of the canteen and print them in our flyers and pamphlets."

Curt was beaming.

All the Schmidts joined in to help with the Children's Canteen Christmas party. Papa had been more than a little impressed by the Uelands, and he felt his family should show their appreciation. Elsa asked Papa to be the one to tell the Christmas story to the children. He accepted with pleasure.

At the Christmas party, Torvald and Curt got to know one another better. As soon as Torvald learned that Curt loved horses, he invited Curt to come out to their place and ride the pony. "When it warms up, that is," Torvald added. "We'd love to have you come."

Curt didn't say much except to mumble his thanks, but Maria knew that inside, Curt was turning handsprings with excitement.

No one thought the war in Europe would last into 1915. Surely, people said, civilized Europeans could stop the conflict through discussions. It might be "peace without victory," but at least it would be peace.

But it was not to be. After Christmas the war turned ugly. Uglier than anyone could have imagined. The Germans launched airships called zeppelins, which dropped bombs on cities such as London and Paris. Death rained down out of the skies on innocent people.

Again and again, Maria and her brothers would ask Papa, "How can this be? Why would Berlin allow such terrible killing?"

But Papa had no answers. He would only shake his head and say, "I do not know, my children. I do not know."

President Wilson made a speech in which he declared to the American people, "This is a war with which we have nothing to do."

Maria didn't mean to be so presumptuous as to contradict the president of the United States, but whether she liked it or not, this war seemed to have a great deal to do with her. Every day she and other German-Americans were taking the brunt of the blame for all that was happening.

Her eighth-grade year was filled with days of stress and unpleasant incidents. However, following the demonstration at the *Tribune*, the atmosphere in the classroom altered somewhat. A reporter from the *Journal* happened upon the scene and took several photos, one of which appeared on their second page the very next day. The photo showed Maria and Thomas standing on the front steps of the *Tribune* building with Mrs. Ueland, Mr. Dalhart, Tony, and Liver Lid. No matter what other students thought of Maria's involvement, it was a matter of some importance to have your picture in the city newspaper.

The other thing that happened at school was that Torvald began talking to Maria. On the playground, Torvald often sought out Curt and talked to him as well. Torvald's attention to the Schmidts seemed to help cool the animosity of the others.

When spring arrived, Curt was given permission on two different Saturdays to visit the Uelands. Of course he took his camera. When he arrived home, he was more talkative than he'd been in many months. Torvald and Rolf had let him forgo the pony and graduated him instead to the big horse. If someone had given Curt a million dollars, Maria knew he wouldn't have been happier than he was to have had a chance to ride that horse.

At long last the month of May arrived. Maria would graduate in just a few weeks. She felt she'd just come through the longest year of her entire life. Then on May 2, news came that rocked the nation to its very core. The fastest, the largest, the most luxurious ocean liner afloat, a British steamer called the *Lusitania,* was torpedoed by a German U-boat and sank just off the coast of Ireland.

Curt read the article aloud while Maria and Thomas folded the papers on that balmy May morning. The account told how the ship went down so quickly that only half the lifeboats could be deployed. Out of twelve hundred passengers, only about seven hundred were saved. Of those who died, sixty-three were children and thirty-one were infants.

Maria wanted Curt to stop reading. She wanted to hold her ears. The very thought of such destruction made her feel sick to her stomach.

Thomas stood to his feet and hoisted his canvas bag over his shoulder. He wasn't smiling. Grimly, he said, "Something tells me this is going to be a very long war. And something tells me America cannot escape being a part of it."

CHAPTER 19

Making a Difference

The hallways leading into the school auditorium were full to overflowing. Maria waited with her graduating classmates. In a few moments they would form lines to make their grand entrance. Maria felt positively elegant in the white dress Elsa had allowed her to borrow.

"This one is to be borrowed," Elsa had told her with a smile. "All three of us girls were graduated in this dress, and Mama is quite partial to it."

Maria tried to talk Elsa out of it, but in the end, even Mrs. Ueland had insisted that Maria wear it. "Since I'll be attending the graduation," the kind lady said, "it would do me proud to see that dress being worn one more time."

From inside the auditorium, Maria heard the music starting to play. Just then, someone tapped her on the shoulder. She turned around to see Cathy Wyatt. Beside her was her mother, who was saying, "So you're the one. You're the Schmidt girl."

Maria looked up at this lady dressed in a gauzy silk dress and large hat smothered in ostrich plumes. Beside her, the cocky Cathy was not so cocky anymore. She was staring at the floor.

"Yes, ma'am?" Maria said.

"I was right there that day at the *Tribune* just before Christmas! Yes, I was. I was one of Clara Ueland's newest recruits. I serve on the city kindergarten committee, you know. I saw you step right up there and go inside with those businessmen. Not a bit afraid. Just like you'd been doing that all your life. I've been telling Cathy all these months that I was *longing* to meet you."

She reached out and took Maria's hand. "Such a strong young thing you are and so determined. I read how you went into the Flats to quell a riot, you brave girl you. I can see now why Elsa and her mother speak highly of you."

She glanced down at her own daughter. "My, how I've encouraged Cathy to stand up for what she believes in. 'Cathy,' I say, 'you should be more like this Schmidt girl.'"

"Excuse me," Maria interrupted her. "I think my brother needs me." Thomas was waving to her from down the hall. "It was nice meeting you, Mrs. Wyatt," Maria said. "Now, if you'll excuse me."

Cathy looked up briefly, and their eyes met. Maria smiled, and Cathy smiled back.

When Maria came up beside Thomas, he said, "What was that all about?"

Maria glanced back to where Cathy was standing. "I'm not sure, but I think the Lord just vindicated me."

On cue, the 1915 graduating class of Washington Elementary School marched into the auditorium singing "America the Beautiful."

"*O beautiful for spacious skies,*" Maria sang, "*for amber waves of grain. . .*"

In the audience, Mama and Papa were sitting right next to Mr. and Mrs. Andreas Ueland. Rolf sat beside Thomas. And on the other side of Mama and Papa sat Aunt Josephine and Uncle Robert and the three cousins, then Curt and Libby. Elsa had come as well and brought along her older sister, Anne.

"*For purple mountain majesties above the fruited plain.*"

Had it been only a year ago that Maria was wishing she were a boy and not a girl? That seemed so far away now.

"*America! America! God shed His grace on thee.*"

The class filled the stage and stood at their places. The richness of the song wrapped around Maria like a sweet perfume and drenched her in patriotic pride.

Since the war had broken out, she'd sometimes wished she were not German. But then she had only to think of her loving papa. She would never wish that he were not her papa, no matter what. If she were German because of him, then so be it. Above all, she knew she was a proud American.

It didn't matter if she were a boy or girl, or if she were German or not. It didn't even matter if she were wealthy or not so wealthy. All that really mattered was that she followed God's will and remained true to His leading.

Maria had no control over what the Germans were doing across the Atlantic. But she was determined to make a difference right where she was. Right here. Right now. Today.

"And crown thy good with brotherhood from sea to shining sea."

If you enjoyed

Maria
Takes a Stand

be sure to read other

SISTERS IN TIME

books from BARBOUR PUBLISHING

- Perfect for Girls Ages Eight to Twelve

- History and Faith in Intriguing Stories

- Lead Character Overcomes Personal Challenge

- Covers Seventeenth to Twentieth Centuries

- Collectible Series of Titles

6" x 8 ¼" / Paperback / 144 pages / $3.97